D1496755

First published 2003 by Zipper Books,
part of Millivres Prowler Limited,
Spectrum House, 32-34 Gordon House Road, London NW5 1LP
www.zipper.co.uk

Copyright © 2003 Turner Kane

Turner Kane has asserted his right to be identified as the author of this work in accordance with the Copyright,
Designs and Patents Act 1988

A catalogue record for this book is available from the British Library

ISBN 1-873741-85-5

Distributed in the UK and Europe by Airlift Book Company,
8 The Arena, Mollison Avenue, Enfield, Middlesex EN3 7NJ
Telephone: 020 8804 0400
Distributed in North America by Consortium,
1045 Westgate Drive, St Paul, MN 55114-1065
Telephone: 1 800 283 3572
Distributed in Australia by Bulldog Books,
PO Box 300, Beaconsfield, NSW 2014

Printed and bound in Finland by WS Bookwell

PERFECT TACKLE

TURNER KANE

Zipper Books

One

Guy Holbrook was bored. It was midweek in the final moments of another working day and he was spending his time avoiding what little he had left to do. For the past five minutes or so he'd been entertaining himself with the catapult he'd made out of a rubber band and his fingers, firing paper clips into the metal bin that sat in the corner of the room. It was the twenty-third attempt when he finally heard the ping of success and raised his arms in elation.

Suddenly, he was back on the pitch, basking in the imaginary cheers of fans ecstatic that he'd sent another one over the crossbar. There were large-chested, broad-shouldered men grabbing at his body in congratulation, the bare skin of their legs brushing against his own, faces – some handsome, some rough and bearing wounds – pressing their lips onto his cheeks. Guy found himself staring at the clock again, having lost himself in his thoughts. There was still half an hour to go before he could leave his office without looking too much as if he was skiving and, though thirty minutes was no time at all in the great scheme of things, it seemed like far too long to wait for someone who was as bored as Guy was at that moment.

He had walked into the position of junior executive in a major IT firm in London straight out of university, thanks to a friend of the family who owned the business and who had pulled some strings for him. At first, Guy had been grateful for the nepotism. The salary was great, bringing in more than enough to maintain the standard of living he was accustomed to as the product of a well-to-do family. He had a decent apartment in the city, a sports car that was only a year old and a wardrobe that was admirably modern and stylish. But after a few months of the dry work he was given to do at the company, the money seemed little compensation and he began to wonder whether he was in the right field at all. For all its economic benefits, the job just didn't stretch him enough. Too many days were spent on mundane, almost pointless tasks and Guy knew he was too young to feel so stifled. He was twenty-two, his body was fit and at its peak and he'd acquired a 2:1 after three years' study at his degree – proving that he was far from stupid. But all this was going to waste and too often of late he felt idle and claustrophobic, like a horse kept too long in the stable. He had become increasingly needy for something that used his body to its full extent, concentrated his mind and excited him.

Guy knew there were only two things that could really draw upon him in such a manner. The first of these was rugby. He was the fly half for Albridge Rugby Union team and it was on the pitch that he felt truly alive; the game called on his intellectual, instinctual and physical skills to ensure the success of his side. He thrilled at being stretched to his limits in the mud and cold, ending a game aching, battered and at the point of exhaustion but feeling distinctly aware of his abilities and achievements. And, as much as he got out of the rugby itself, he got an equal amount out of knowing others through the sport, of being part of a team. He found the camaraderie that existed between himself and his fellow players brought some of the greatest happiness in his life, and often overlapped into his other main passion.

For Guy loved sex as much as he loved rugby, and he found the men that surrounded him on the pitch, in the baths or in the bar after the match attractive in the extreme. Sometimes he would be so turned on by having hard, sweaty bodies wrapped around him, seeing the glimpses of thick legs in muddy shorts or being scrubbed clean by one of his buddies, that he could barely stop himself from acting on his desires. It was only the fact that he had had a steady boyfriend for some time that prevented him from doing so. Yes, it was sport and men that made the electricity of life bolt through him, that made him feel wonderfully young and vital. Next to these two passions, sitting behind a keyboard all day just couldn't compare.

A loud voice broke Guy's thoughts and his office door was suddenly flung open.

"Well, balls to him being busy. I'm going in anyway!" It was Hugo, Guy's boyfriend, his School Prefect intonations dominating and determined over the protests of the poor secretary. He stormed into the room, then slammed the door behind him.

"Holbrook! Idling as usual, eh? Well, sir, make yourself busy."

Guy got up from his swivel chair and loosely took hold of Hugo to kiss him. As he did so, he got a faint whiff of alcohol on the man's breath.

"Drunk again?" he asked, feeling like a scolding parent.

"Barely," Hugo boomed. "Just a couple to prepare me for what lies ahead." He half-sat, half-leant on Guy's desk. "Another bloody family gathering. You'd think I'd have run out of cousins who need to be formally introduced to the world."

"Who is it this time?" Guy popped his head out of the office to shrug an apology at his assistant.

"Someone twice removed on my mother's side. You don't know her. *I* don't know her, for Christ's sake, but it'll be the same sort of thing as usual. Sweet sixteen and never been kissed, trying to find her an eligible bachelor and all that balls. Don't worry, I told them you were working late." Hugo took Guy's place at the desk. He switched on the computer to play with the mouse. "I think I'll be slipping away before the night's over. Don't fancy wasting a decent stupor on those bloody stiffs."

Guy plumped himself down in the chair on the opposite side of the desk. He watched Hugo shaking his floppy fringe out of his eyes as the computer made its familiar beeping noises in connecting to its server.

"What's the plan, then?" he asked. "For after the party, I mean."

Hugo looked surprised. "But it's Wednesday! I thought you'd be working tomorrow."

"I might be out of a job if I keep allowing my drunken friends to burst in to interrupt my busy schedule."

"I'm merely tiddly. And sorry, darling, but I've arranged to meet Kier and Cassandra and I'm not sure where we'll end up. I'll ring you if you like."

Guy groaned inwardly at the thought of Hugo's dullard friends. "I just remembered. Bit of a conference in the morning. Wouldn't want to turn up looking like I was hung over."

"It's up to you." Hugo turned his attentions to the computer again and was busily typing something into it. Guy could tell Hugo wasn't overly bothered that he wouldn't be out that night. Too often of late he seemed to be playing second fiddle to Hugo's other interests. He took the brief pause in the conversation to begin to wonder about their relationship. Hugo was undeniably attractive. His blond hair was long at the front and it had a slight curl in it that gave him a tousled look as if he had just got out of bed. He had a strong jaw line, perfect skin and teeth and a tall, well-built body. His demeanour was cocky and confident. He had the personality of someone not afraid for his voice to be overheard complaining in a restaurant and it had been developed over a lifetime of nannies, servants and public schools. Hugo had once confessed that he had been the school bully at prep school and Guy could well believe it. Now, as a young adult, Hugo's character was striking, sometimes overbearing, but definitely magnetic. However, despite how attractive Guy found his lover, something of late was taking the edge off their relationship.

Hugo was the product of a rich businessman father and a woman with a minor title. Guy couldn't quite remember what the connection was between Hugo's parents and his own, but it had led to the invitation to the dinner party where he and Hugo had first met. They had been seated together at the table on their first collision, it being assumed that, as they were the same age, they would get along. The attraction on Guy's side had been immediate, although it lessened as Hugo's boorishness became more obtrusive. Guy grew more and more unsettled as Hugo became louder and louder, drinking far too much too fast and starting to insult the other guests around them, embarrassing both Guy and his own parents. The scene eventually came to a head when Hugo, being over-demonstrative in the middle of another childish quip, fell backwards off his chair, pulling what was left of his main course all over his tuxedo. The action made him the centre of attention for the last time that evening. His mother apologised for his behaviour, then politely asked Guy to help him clean up. Guy acquiesced rather reluctantly, hooking the young drunk under his arm, by that point not harbouring any desire to baby-sit someone who was such an attention-seeking fool.

Hugo was sniggering and burping as Guy dumped him on the bed of the nearest guest room. He became rather unco-operative as Guy started to help him out of his clothes, wriggling out of his grasp as Guy tried to remove his jacket, batting Guy's hands away as he tugged his bow tie undone. He only settled down as Guy began to unbutton his dress shirt, lying back as if to go to sleep. Guy began to feel aroused as Hugo's fresh, taut skin gradually came into view. He made a conscious effort to steel himself and, ignoring his desires, concentrated on the matter in hand.

"Are you always such a brat?" he asked sternly as he tugged the shirt out from Hugo's trousers. It was a rhetorical question more than anything and he'd not expected much of a response but, to his surprise, Hugo sat up suddenly and began smiling.

"I don't know," he said, apparently lucid again. "Are you always so handsome?"

He lunged, planting a forceful kiss directly on Guy's lips. He laughed as Guy struggled against his naked torso and it was at that moment that Guy realised Hugo was barely drunk at all. His bad behaviour had simply been an act.

"These dinners are so bloody boring," Hugo explained as he unbuckled his belt. "I just had to get out of there somehow and do something a bit more exciting."

The two made love there and then. Later, to cover his lengthy absence from the dinner table, Guy had lied to his parents, saying that Hugo had simply been too ill to be left alone. He knew right from that night that Hugo was wild and reckless. He grew to realise his new boyfriend was also rather spoilt, coming from such a wealthy family and being the recipient of a large trust fund that was keeping him out of work and in various bars around London. It was these characteristics that had at first made him seem dangerous, a little immature, but very attractive. Lately, however, they were slowly becoming more wearing and tiresome. Hugo's devil-may-care attitude made him irresponsible and unreliable and he had let Guy down so often recently that Guy had begun to wonder when the man would finally grow up. His slightly sozzled entry into the office that afternoon had just made his point of maturation seem a long, long way off.

"Found the bastard!" Hugo finishing his clicking and turned the terminal around so that Guy could see it. A pixelated photograph slowly came into view. It depicted two handsome, burly men sitting on a bench in what seemed to be a changing room. They wore rugby shirts and, from the muddy state of their legs, had obviously just been playing a game. They had removed their shorts and their thighs were splayed to reveal two large-sized erections. The men were grinning as if rather pleased to display their trophies. The shot looked candid, unprofessional, as if it might even have been a couple of straight guys mucking around rather than proper photography and it turned Guy on immediately.

"This internet malarkey is pretty amazing," Hugo nodded at the screen. "In terms of porn, it's better than videotape. Anyway, is this anyone you know?"

"I wish," said Guy. "Maybe they're Aussies. I don't recognise the strip."

"The chap on the left reminded me of you," Hugo beamed.

Guy looked closer at the man. He was dark and stocky, not fat but of a naturally big build. His thighs were bulky and hairy and his looks were cheekily boyish. Guy felt rather complimented by the comparison.

"So, is that the kind of stuff you get up to after a match?"

"Not quite." Guy remembered a few times when his team-mates' playfulness in the bath after a match had teetered on the brink of becoming more than simply messing around, but it had never gone so far as what he could see on the screen at that moment.

"Good. I'm glad."

Guy looked up, surprised at a rare display of what seemed to be jealousy from Hugo, but then the statement was quickly clarified.

"I thought I might have to start taking more of an interest in the game."

That was more like the Hugo Guy knew; by that point, however, he had developed other things on his mind than Hugo's flippancy. He was horny and he guessed Hugo felt the same way.

"So, you have a thing for rugby players then?" he teased.

The material at his crotch felt constricted and tangled from the increase in its contents and he pulled at it slightly, shuffling what was inside to manoeuvre it into a more comfortable position.

"A thing for rugby players? I guess you could say that." Hugo stood up and walked around the desk. The front of his trousers was bulging as he positioned himself in front of Guy. "Why, do you want to see it?"

Hugo traced the tips of his fingers down the outline of his erection, before giving the end a good squeeze.

"Not here, Hugo." Guy felt suddenly wary. "It's too risky. Someone might walk in on us."

Hugo lunged over the desk and pulled Guy closer to him, so close that Guy could feel his hot, panting breath on his cheek. Their lips came closer and, in spite of his desire, Guy readied himself to push Hugo off. Then at the last second, Hugo turned and instead reached over his boyfriend.

Guy heard a click as Hugo pressed a button on his intercom.

"Private meeting," he said, obviously attempting to approximate Guy's deep, commanding voice. "Make sure we're not disturbed for a while."

"Er... Yes, Mr Holbrook." Guy's secretary sounded a little confused and the two men laughed. Guy arched back, preparing to go and explain that it had all been a little joke, but Hugo grabbed hold of his arms and pinned him to the desk. Guy struggled at first and then, his lust feeling too good to be ignored, he acquiesced.

"Oh, you're a naughty boy." Guy smiled.

Hugo eased himself downwards slightly. "And don't you just love it," he said cockily.

Hugo nuzzled Guy's face a couple of times, brushing noses, pulling away if Guy's lips got too close before finally making contact.

If there was one thing that just about made up for all Hugo's shortcomings as a boyfriend, it was that as a lover he knew exactly what to do. He was surely the best kisser Guy had ever known. Guy forgot he was at work and simply slipped into the pleasures of those lips upon him. Soon enough, a tongue was wriggling into his mouth, dancing over his own with confident, eager strokes. He accepted more of it into him, until his entire gullet seemed filled with the warm, wet flesh. Then, just as his passions and pulse were reaching a high point, Hugo pulled away.

"Are you going to play nicely or am I going to have to hold you down till we're done?" he asked. He was obviously only half-joking.

Guy wanted Hugo so badly he would have agreed to just about anything. "I'll play... play nicely," he panted.

"All right, then." Stepping back slightly, Hugo fiddled with his trousers, before yanking them and his underwear downwards to his calves. "How about you play with this?"

Hugo's dick bounced around in its sudden freedom, lifting the hemline of his shirt so that the crisp, white material draped down like theatre curtains at either side. It created as gorgeous a sight as it ever had. Hugo had the kind of prick that reflected its owner's self-assurance: thick, just over eight inches long and with a good bulbous head. Its foreskin never rolled fully back without aid, instead forming a circle of skin at the end through which peeped an almost blood-red glans and a slit much deeper and darker than any others Guy had come across, even in pornography. It was a proud, manly thing that Hugo was never ashamed of showing off or using. It looked incongruous, but fantastic exposed against its owner's expensive clothes and Guy just had to bring it close to him.

He ran his hand up Hugo's thighs, taking a good squeeze of the hardy muscles just above the knees, feeling the fine coating of blond hairs upon his fingers, enjoying Hugo's shiver as his palms reached the insides of his legs. He placed one hand right at the top, at the hairy passageway leading to Hugo's behind before taking Hugo's balls into his palm and fondling them with care. They, too, were furry and he tickled his fingers along the saggy wrinkled skin, knowing, after many experiences before, just how much joy his lover got from being touched like that.

"Not rugby balls, but they'll do, eh?" Hugo murmured , his eyes closed.

"Damn right they will." With his free hand, Guy at last took hold of the engorged thing that pointed at him inches from his face. He clenched it hard and Hugo gasped. He dragged its skin towards him, watching as its deep hollows filled up with the shiny pre-come he was forcing out of it. The foreskin rose up fully in a pocket of wrinkles, a warm drip oozing outwards and onto Guy's hand before he pushed back again. Slowly, more and more of the round head could be seen until Guy had exposed it all, its unusual, truly helmet-like shape growing and shrinking slightly with every throb of the tower that it topped. Guy dipped his middle finger into its dampened indent and, coaxing out some more man-lube, gently wiped it all over the first inch or so of Hugo's prick.

"Oh..." Hugo was obviously enjoying himself greatly, but his next comment revealed how ready he was. "Come on, you bastard, do it for me properly."

Once more, Guy grabbed at the thing, Hugo sucking air through his teeth in pleasure as he did so. He began to wank fully, slowly at first, never letting his tight grip lessen as he moved his hand back and forth. Gradually, he increased his speed, still holding Hugo's balls in his other hand as his regular, jerking wrist movements became more and more rapid. Guy loved having a piece of hard meat in his hand, how it pulsated again and again as if struggling against him. It felt like nothing else to be found on a human body, not mere flesh or bone, just one hundred per cent masculine muscle. The length he held at that moment looked so good. It was dribbling quite readily and, suddenly feeling hungry, Guy moved in to take a taste.

Looking upwards into his lover's eyes, he extended his tongue.

"Oh, that's it, you beautiful horny bastard," Hugo mumbled. "Lick me like a dog."

Happy to do exactly as he was told, Guy rasped right up from the thing's thick base to its very tip, causing Hugo to release a guttural moan. Guy dragged his tongue over the end, getting a full blast of the distinctive manly taste of his lover. Steadying the thing with one hand, he licked around and around it before enclosing it within the tunnel made by his lips. He couldn't help but be aroused by the obvious rapture he was producing in his boyfriend and he paused a moment to enjoy Hugo's groans before taking a handful of his own genitals and giving them a rub.

Just at that moment, the office intercom on Guy's desk beeped. At first, he ignored it and continued what he was doing but the machine resonated again and again so insistently that he had to pull away.

"Balls to that," Hugo grumbled. "Tell her where she can shove her internal memos."

"I'll just be a second," Guy said, reaching backwards to press the 'speak' button. "Yes, Fiona."

"Sorry, Mr Holbrook, I know you said you weren't to be disturbed but the man on the end of the line says it's rather urgent."

"Don't worry, Fiona. Put it through." Though he would have much preferred to carry on with Hugo, he knew he couldn't and shouldn't let the call pass.

"You'd better make it quick," Hugo instructed. "I don't feel patient."

Guy picked up the handset. "Holbrook," he said, trying to reconstruct his mind into a state able to cope with business.

"All right there, Guy?" The voice on the end of the line had a northern accent and it was one that Guy didn't recognise. "I've been trying to get hold of you for some time. My name's Ron Lambert. I'm the manager for Welby. I think you should have heard of us."

Guy was surprised. He *had* heard of Welby. It was a small town in the north of England that had an excellent Rugby League team.

"I'll get straight to the point," Lambert continued. "I've had my eye on you for some time. To play for Welby, I mean. And I'd like to arrange a meeting to discuss it."

"Really?" Guy felt quite honoured. Despite his talents, he hadn't suspected anyone outside the Rugby Union world had taken much interest in his sporting career.

"It'd mean a lot of changes, of course. Turning professional, moving up here. The pay packet might be some compensation, though we can talk about that when I see you."

Professional rugby was exactly the kind of challenge Guy needed in his life.

"Right." He pretended to be calm. "I'll check my diary."

A time and a place were arranged for the weekend, phone numbers and platitudes exchanged. The call over and feeling both stunned and elated, Guy replaced the handset.

"What?" Hugo looked slightly confused. His erection had lessened in ferocity and now dangled slightly, still thickened but only half-aroused.

Guy launched himself at his boyfriend, picked up him in a big bear hug and spun him around, laughing and cheering.

"Damn it, man!" Hugo stumbled as Guy placed him back down, his partially removed trousers causing him to lose his balance slightly. But he still raised a smile at the sudden attack and his boyfriend's elation.

"It's Welby, you know, the League team," Guy explained. "They want me to sign for them, turn pro."

He clarified further, going through what his potential future had in store.

"I'd get to play a lot more, of course. And best of all, I'd be rid of this bloody job." He swept his arm around to indicate his office.

"That's fantastic!" Hugo's smile lingered for a moment, before a sudden thought struck him and he went quiet. "You'd move away, of course."

It was the first time Guy saw the effect it would have on their relationship. Unless Hugo moved with him, they would undoubtedly be seeing less of each other in the future.

"Not necessarily," he began, not entirely convinced by what he was saying himself.

"Oh, sod it," Hugo returned to his usual resilient self. "It's great news. Let's not spoil it."

He grabbed hold of Guy once more. Guy could feel the man's semi-hard genitals pressing against his crotch.

"Let's fucking celebrate."

"And how are we going to do that?" Guy asked innocently.

"I don't know." Hugo dropped to a kneeling position, his face at the level of Guy's crotch. "Any suggestions?"

He unzipped Guy's trousers. Guy felt Hugo's hand delve inside and begin feeling around. His prick surged with blood as Hugo pulled the waistband of his brief-pants down underneath his balls so that his genitalia popped out unrestricted. Guy liked how he looked like that. Just as when he had seen Hugo's dick next to his tuxedo, he enjoyed how his own parts looked somehow wrong, but still sexy poking out of his expensive black trousers. There were tufts of black hair sticking out at either side of the base that seemed to accentuate the thing's rawness. Guy watched the tree-like pattern of blue veins pumping blood into his cock's dark brown skin with every pull Hugo made on it. Soon it grew to its full seven inches, not as long as Hugo's or as thick, but still, as Guy knew, a respectable size. Like Hugo, Guy was uncircumcised, but his foreskin rolled back of its own accord once full erection had been achieved and now his deep red, oval bell end trembled at the side of Hugo's cheek as he felt his balls being massaged.

"So, sir, since it's your special day, any requests?"

Guy could feel his lover's breath buffet against his exposed skin as he spoke.

"The usual, I think," he joked.

Hugo raised an eyebrow. "It'll be my pleasure."

He opened his mouth and Guy watched briefly as his cock was enveloped, then closed his eyes as the damp, heated hollow engulfed him entirely. He sensed he was deep within Hugo's throat, feeling Hugo's chin against his balls. His hard piece juddered involuntarily and he wondered if Hugo could feel the shaky movements within him. Hugo pulled back and Guy gasped at the exquisite rubbing sensation of the rough, saliva-coated tongue on the underneath of his hard-on. Then, with the kind of noise someone makes on tasting well-cooked food, Hugo slid back down. Guy watched the man's cheeks indent as he sucked. The action was repeated a few times: Guy's body felt at once stiffened, heightened, relaxed and enraptured with pleasure. He put his hands on Hugo's strong shoulders, then entangled his fingers into the man's hair, enjoying the feeling of having a handsome head between his legs. Then, after what seemed like far too short a time, he released his load into Hugo's mouth.

"That do you, Holbrook?" Hugo was panting as he spoke and Guy noticed he was yanking his own engorged prick quite readily.

"That was exactly what I had in mind," Guy said gratefully.

"Good." Hugo removed Guy's trousers with little care, pulling them down in a strong, brusque manner. "Turn around. I've got the taste for you now."

Guy did as he was told. He leant across his desk, shuffled his legs apart as far as the constrictions of his clothing would allow. He felt tender kisses on his buttocks and on the tops of his thighs, then groaned as Hugo bit into the tender flesh. He felt a wet probing thing at the top of his buttocks. He knew it to be Hugo's tongue and, needing to feel more of it, he reached back and pulled apart his arsecheeks. He felt the probe easing gently downwards, then hit the bull's-eye and begin wriggling around. There was a tickling, itching sensation as it danced upon him, its tip drawing around and around his anus before forcefully but tenderly moving inwards. Guy murmured his boyfriend's name as he was at last opened and he felt himself being pleasantly filled by the writhing insertion. The thing waited momentarily before it began prodding, exiting then re-entering him with sure strokes. Guy's nerve-endings rewarded him with waves of ecstasy at being pampered like that. He became more excited, his heartbeat increasing at the pleasure he was feeling and the knowledge that he was being primed for a more complete coupling. Soon enough, the tongue was removed and, after a couple of full, lengthy laps that really moistened his crack, Hugo stood up behind him.

"I've never dined out anywhere better." Hugo leant over him and Guy could feel the man's hard-on slide in between his legs, feeling steely and hot against his balls.

"Well, you've had the meal," Guy panted. "Now how's about a show?"

He was still wearing his jacket. He delved in the inside pocket and took out a condom and a packet of lube he kept there for such emergencies.

"It's a good job I like you for your arse and not your sense of humour." Hugo accepted the gifts.

Guy heard rustling behind him as the packets were ripped open. His dick throbbed as Hugo's lubricated fingers stroked his crack firmly, then invaded him with determination. They poked at him a few times, introducing him to the familiar, always welcome mixture of thrilling pain and wondrous sensation, until Hugo checked his boyfriend's readiness.

"Bloody hell, yes," Guy encouraged. "Get it inside me."

There was a pressure of something far larger than anything else that had been up there that day trying to get in him. He could feel his hole struggle against it, then as he relaxed, gradually stretch open. Inch by inch, the hardened man-meat forced its way upward, causing Guy to lose his breath with its encroachment, until it was fully inside him. Hugo had hold of him tightly, his mouth kissing at his neck, sometimes letting out unconscious, uncontrolled utterances as the two took time to become accustomed to the coupling.

"Fuck me, Hugo," Guy begged. "I want to feel your cock pummelling my arse."

Hugo did as he was told and gave the first slow shunt. Both men moaned at the movement, then again at the second which was harder and more assured. Guy pushed back to meet his lover's strokes, his arse muscles relenting as the fucks became faster, until the slap, slap, slap of their bodies together was as regular and determined as the ticking of the clock on the office wall. Guy felt Hugo's hand wander over his chest and belly, then down to where his member bounced and jiggled with every pound his backside took. The hand grabbed hold of him. It began to jerk him off and he rose to new levels of pleasure as it did so. Being taken like that was one of Guy's greatest joys, the physical and mental sensation of having a man all over, wanting him, penetrating him with near bestial actions. He squeezed his insides tighter as their bucking reached a peak, Hugo literally dragging him backwards onto the hardest, fullest shafts he could take. He heard Hugo mumble a warning and then felt the thing up him go off, vibrating again and again against his chute as the orgasm possessed it. Then, unable to take any more he, too, relinquished hold on himself. His dick was the only thing on his mind, and the pleasure it provided spread quickly over his entire body as it thickened to its maximum hardness, then began to pump. His body convulsed as Hugo finally brought him off, his white spray shooting all over his desk, squirting over Hugo's fingers, some drops flying onto the front of his shirt as his rectum clenched violently against Hugo's prick. Gradually, the climax lessened and he felt warm and at peace. Slightly exhausted, he felt Hugo remove himself so they could turn to face each other once more.

"Well, as celebrations go, that was one of the best I've had," Guy said, satisfied. He pulled up his trousers, the sweat on his groin moist against his underwear. "And healthier for you than a night on the booze."

"Speaking of which," Hugo pulled off his condom with a thwack. His dick, now growing flaccid, still looked gorgeous, shiny as it was with a coating of its own come. "I'd better get a move on. I'm supposed to be there at 6.30." He wiped himself with a handkerchief, then got dressed.

"Love you, leave you, sir," Hugo gave Guy a quick peck on the cheek then, whistling a classical tune, strode towards the door.

"I'll speak to you soon," Guy said in return. "Enjoy tonight."

Still whistling, Hugo simply rolled his eyes, then winked as he left.

Guy returned to his seat at the desk. He wondered if Hugo knew how cold his behaviour could seem sometimes, how abrupt his departure had been, mere moments after the two of them had made love. He began to feel a little empty, then quickly dismissed his ponderings. Hugo was as 'Hugo' ever was. Self-centred, but rather beautiful and with sexual abilities Guy was more than happy with. His afterglow creating a peacefulness within him, Guy shut down his computer and readied himself to leave. The combination of great sex and a life-changing possibility on the horizon had cheered him and he left the office thinking how the afternoon had not turned out to be such a bad one after all.

Two

Guy had just ordered a coffee when he saw Lambert walk in. The man looked a little lost, so Guy stood up and gave him a wave. Lambert's face broke into a big grin and he strode over to the table.

"There you are!" He stuck out a hefty hand. "Pleased to meet you at last."

Guy met the man's grip. The handshake was strong and warm.

"Same here. Good to put a face to the voice on the end of the line."

"Knew your face already, of course." Lambert took off his heavy overcoat and sat down. "Seen it on TV enough. That's where I spotted you. I'll tell you now, you don't half look good on the screen."

Lambert was still smiling. He had a slightly weathered but appealingly broad face and he looked somewhere in his early forties. His hair had turned a dark grey and his eyes were a pure light blue. His body was of a larger build than average, but he fitted his suit well and had taken a relaxed pose in his chair that indicated he was completely comfortable within it.

"Thanks." Guy wondered if Lambert had picked up on his staring. He felt slightly taken with the masculine-looking older man. "Before we get down to business, can I get you a drink?"

"Thought you'd never ask." Lambert's voice was deep and it rumbled with rolling, northern vowels. "I'm parched. What're you having?

"Just a latte. I'm driving."

"Well, I'll wet the baby's head for the both of us. Mine's a pint of bitter, if they've got it."

Guy laughed. He caught the attention of a waiter and asked for the drink.

"Classy place, this." Lambert was looking around at the brightly lit, modern design of the café bar. "Nice view, as well." He nodded towards the large windows that overlooked the Thames. "You won't find much like this in Welby, you know that."

Guy nodded. "Don't worry. I think I'm ready for a change."

"Good. Because what else we have to offer a player as talented as you will make your life in union seem like something out of the Dark Ages."

Lambert leaned across the table, now serious and determined. Guy could instantly feel the man was a talker. He was coming across like a salesman for the benefits of League rugby, going over once more the differences Guy would find if he turned professional. Guy actually needed little convincing. He had already made up his mind that he would take whatever offer Welby gave him, within reason. But he didn't interrupt. Lambert obviously had such a love of the game that enthusing about his team in a passionate manner gave him great enjoyment and Guy didn't feel like cutting short his pleasures.

"... it'll be a test," Lambert surmised, "that'll push you harder physically and mentally than ever before. You'll be training a lot more, for a start. But I've seen what you're like on the pitch. You've got that yearning, that fire in your eyes. You're determined and I know Welby will be exactly what you want."

Lambert picked up his pint and took his first sip since it had arrived. "And don't you worry about living up North," he continued. "Welby might be a tiny place compared to what you're used to here, but what it lacks in size it makes up for with its sense of community. People know each other there, people *care*. The team's important to them and I just want to know if you're ready to become part of it all."

"Let's talk about money." Guy changed the subject. In reality, the money was one of the last reasons he had already decided to play for Welby, but he didn't want to look foolhardy or let Lambert think he had him on a plate.

Lambert laughed heartily, throwing his head back in a manly gesture that Guy found undeniably attractive.

"You're a shrewd lad, Holbrook. Remind me of myself a good fifteen years ago. And I'll tell you now, the Board weren't as generous when they took me on then as they are being with you."

He paused as if weighing up the man in front of him, staring Guy directly in the eye.

"How does seventy grand sound?" he said at last. "Twenty grand up front, ten at Christmas, and the rest spread over the next five years."

Guy was impressed. The last Union player he had heard of who had made the switch to League had been offered eighty thousand and that had been a major and important signing. Lambert's offer was a good one and it was at that point that he realised just how much Welby wanted him.

"Seventy?" Guy pulled a face as if he was taking time to consider his options, wanting still to play it cool. He stroked his chin before finally giving an answer. "That doesn't sound too bad."

Lambert laughed again. He thrust forward his hand once more.

"Put it there, pal. I take it that means that it's a deal."

They shook hands, Lambert's clasp firm and authoritative.

"It's a deal, Ron. I'm happy to be onboard."

"That's great, Guy. We're happy to have you." He settled back in his chair. "Right. We can relax a bit now that's over, get to know each other a bit better."

"Sounds good to me. What did you think of my game on Sunday?"

As Lambert began a constructive, critical and emphatic appraisal of Albridge's last match, Guy began to feel more and more lucky. Lambert was a large, handsome chap of the kind Guy liked best, his manliness becoming increasingly accentuated in the confident, eager mannerisms he displayed as he spoke. The man was an out-and-out hunk and, if there were more like him up north, the future in league looked bright indeed – and not only for the opportunities in sport it offered.

"Welby, darling? You surely can't be serious!"

It was Saturday afternoon. Guy had returned to his old home to break the news of his move to his mother and father. He sat facing them in the living room of their country home, leaning over the coffee table on the edge of a large leather armchair. His revelation seemed to be hitting home a lot harder than he had expected. Things had actually gone a lot more smoothly when he had come out to his parents. At this precise moment his mother's expression was one of shock and surprise.

"But it must be so... small there!" Guy's mother had her hand on the pearls she was wearing over her plain green sweater and she twisted them in a gesture of frenzied concern.

Guy couldn't help himself but laugh at her argument. It was such a silly comment to make, but at the same time, he knew what really lay behind it.

"If you mean compared to London, you're right. But then, so is here and I lived here long enough."

His parents' house was in a small village a good half-hour's drive from the nearest town. It was, in fact, a lot smaller than his intended new home. "And maybe I'm tired of big city living."

"Well, I think you'll get claustrophobic after a week." Guy's mother got up, dusted off some imaginary crumbs from her tweed skirt and headed towards the large fireplace that dominated the room. "And you'll have so much trouble fitting in. A place like

22

that just isn't what you're about."

"Like what?" Guy rolled his eyes. Reading between the lines, he knew she saw the move as a social step downwards. "Mother, you've never even been to Welby. How would you know what it's like?"

"What about your job?" Guy's father had been his usual, mostly silent, ruminative self since his son's arrival. His manner was as unshakeable as always and his concerns about Guy's behaviour seemed, as ever, to be practical ones. "Called in a lot of favours to get you that. It's not a position you walk away from lightly."

"Well, you know I'm grateful, but it just wasn't turning out right for me there. It was too undemanding. There was no future. I could find a million jobs like that. But in Welby I've got the opportunity to do something really special with my life."

His mother tutted with overstated despair. She turned to the mantelpiece and picked up a mounted photograph of Guy in his rugby kit, taken many years ago after he had captained a game at boarding school.

"I thought you'd settled down in London," she said forlornly.

Guy looked at her with understanding. His mother was a born worrier, never someone who liked her boat rocking too much. He could tell it was the sense of upheaval that was getting to her more than anything. Now his parents had both retired, he guessed that all she wanted and expected in her life was for everything to appear calm and unchallenging and the fact that her son was making such a big change, moving somewhere that was a lot further away than where he had been living, was a little too much for her. He got out of his armchair, walked over to her and gently clasped her shoulders.

"Don't be like that, Mum. I really want to do this. It feels like what I've been waiting for all my life."

She took hold of his hand and looked at him. She looked tired and a little upset, but there was something in her eyes that told him her defences were breaking slightly.

"Tell her, Dad." He turned to his father, who had put on his glasses in order to fill his pipe. "It's not such a bad idea, is it?"

Guy's father was a stoical man who took great pride in his son's sporting career. Guy hoped that an appeal to him might allay his mother's fears.

"What about the money?" his father asked, taking a packet of tobacco from his cardigan pocket. "That's the important thing. Have they talked to you about that?"

The man was still considered and collected. Over the years, Guy had worked out that it was his years in the army that had made him direct but rather reserved with his emotions. Knowing that the deal Welby had offered him wasn't a bad one, Guy briefly ran over the ins and outs of his contract. To his surprise, his father began grinning in a rare display of spontaneous delight.

"So, yearly, you're not looking at much more than what you're getting at the moment." His father had obviously quickly done the calculations.

"No, but..." Guy was about to say that it wasn't the money that he was interested in when his father interrupted.

"But it's a bloody good package, that's what!" he laughed. "Not many get a deal like that."

Guy's mother turned and gave her husband a disapproving stare. "Henry!" she pleaded, wanting support.

"Oh, come on, Barb. He's just said he's got nothing to lose financially. And look at him, he's not been this excited since he played his first team games." He lit his pipe and took a long puff. "The way I see it, we've got no other choice but to give him our approval. And if not that, at least a decent chance."

"Thanks, Dad." Guy beamed. His father's faith in him had warmed his heart. His mother, however, seemed to be standing fast. She yanked her hand away from his, crossed her arms and petulantly pursed her lips.

Guy looked at her expectantly, and tried to put on his most

earnest look. A few seconds passed before she spoke.

"Oh, all right, but don't say I can't come over all self-righteous when it all goes wrong," she said, mocking herself and her reserve.

Guy hugged her, knowing how grudgingly her endorsement had been given, but appreciating it all the same.

"Well, you know I would have gone ahead and done it whether you had like it or not," he joked with some truth before letting her go.

"Yes, we know." His mother's mood had become less icy, more good-humoured. "But that's not the point."

All three Holbrooks laughed, a family again. Guy's father picked up the paper he had placed on the coffee table on his son's arrival.

"As long as you make us proud," he said over the rustling of the pages. "That's all we ask of you."

Guy felt confident, bolstered by the fact he would leave his family behind in positive spirits.

"I will," he confirmed, confidently. "Don't worry, Dad, I will."

The remainder of the rugby season seemed to pass rather quickly. The period was touched with not a little sadness, despite Guy's eagerness for his relocation. He had made friends at Albridge and there were people there he admired greatly. He enjoyed the comradeship he felt in the team and knew there were bonds and relationships of trust there that he would miss greatly. When the day rolled around that he would play his last game with the team, he felt slightly low, but determined the match would be one to be remembered.

Appropriately, the game was to be played at home. He arrived at the ground at his usual time, but was surprised to find his team-mates already in the changing rooms ready in their kit when he got there. The men went quiet as soon as the door closed behind him and immediately he suspected a trick.

"Well, well, well," Bryan Kent, the team's captain, a hugely-built prop, approached Guy in an aggressive manner. "If it isn't our little deserter."

"Now, now, Bry." Guy guessed that Kent's attempts to intimidate him were actually in good humour, but he couldn't help but become little wary of what the six-foot-five slab of a man had in store for him. "I'm not deserting. I simply got the chance to move up in the world and I took it," he joked, getting a rumble of disapproval from the other men in the room.

"Oh, just too bloody pretty for Union, then?" Kent got closer.

"It was you fellows holding me back that was the real problem," Guy ribbed. The rumble got louder and he heard a few ribald laughs.

"Is that right?" Kent was almost touching Guy with his huge belly, he was now so close. He slid a massive arm around Guy's neck, Guy knowing that to try and squirm away from what his friends had in store would only prolong the torment.

"Well, in spite of your obvious dissatisfaction, we've got together and organised a farewell gift for you." Kent's grasp became a headlock and Guy found himself yanked around a couple of times before being brought around to face his teammates. "Get a load of this, Holbrook. I think you'll enjoy it."

Guy watched, his head pressed tight against Kent's large, hard body as the prime players of Albridge's First XV shuffled themselves into a line and turned their backs towards him. He half guessed what was on the horizon.

"Ready, boys? Kent asked. After receiving replies in the affirmative, he gave the signal. "Right, drop 'em!"

Bending over, the men simultaneously pulled down their shorts and mooned Guy and Kent. Guy couldn't help but laugh as he saw what had been written on the exposed cheeks in black marker. A letter on each buttock of every man spelled out the farewell message "GOOD LUCK YOU BLOODY TRAITOR!".

Although he had seen his buddies naked in the changing rooms many times, something about them being bared like that especially for him began to arouse him. There was a great selection of behinds in that mock scrum, some big and meaty, others more pert and toned, one so hairy he could barely make out the letters on it. All were somehow made the more attractive by being delineated by a rugby shirt above and a pair of shorts, thick socks and boots below. Guy would've enjoyed getting closer to them but, knowing that it was neither the time nor the place, he settled for merely the sight, pleasurable as it was.

"Oh, bloody hell!" Kent exclaimed. "I forgot the camera. Griff, it's in the top of my bag. Throw it to this loser, will you? I'll let him do the honours."

The men kept their positions as Griff, the team's left wing, delved into a sports bag near where he squatted. Guy couldn't help but be delighted by the jiggling of the man's partially split bum as he searched, his hairy balls dangling between the tops of his thick thighs. Just when he thought the view couldn't get any better, Griff stood up and turned, his dark-skinned, flaccid cock brushing against the naked backside of the man next to him.

"Heads up," Griff shouted, pitching the camera across the room with a direct pass.

Still held hard by Kent, Guy caught the disposable machine. Fitting the message in the viewfinder best as he could, he took a couple of shots.

"That's lovely," he said as Kent finally released him. "Just how I'd like to remember you all."

The men roared a cheer as they stood up and covered themselves.

"We'll get a copy done and framed for you," Kent beamed at Guy. "It'll look great on your mantelpiece."

Guy could think of a much better use for the picture but he decided to keep his thoughts to himself. "But you weren't in the line-up!" he exclaimed, disappointed.

Taking the hint, Kent, too, yanked down his shorts. But instead of bending over, he simply stood, unashamed of his nudity.

"I'll tell you what," he said. "I'll pose for you solo."

He put one arm behind his head, lifted up his shirt to reveal his mighty stomach and pouted.

"That's beautiful, Bry." Guy put the camera to his eye once again. "But I could do with a telephoto lens for that thing."

Kent's huge penis matched the rest of the man's body in its larger-than-average size. Though flaccid, it looked as big as most men's did when erect and its head rested on the elastic waistband of Kent's shorts. Kent was unsurprisingly proud of his manhood and he was always one to show it off in the showers or, more inappropriately, when drunk in the pub after a match. Guy had always found the sight of the thing enticing merely because of its size and appreciated the chance to peruse it properly.

"Now I'll really look forward to getting that one developed," he winked as Kent manoeuvred his packet undercover once more.

"I bet you will, you dirty bastard!" Kent whacked Guy's behind with one of his brawny paws. "Now get changed. It may be your last game with Albridge but I want you playing like it was your first."

"Yes, sir!" Guy did as he was told, his spirits raised by his friends' jovial horseplay.

The match went well, with Guy overjoyed at Albridge's respectable win. He felt he played as good a game as he ever had, scoring several tries in the process. He was glad to be leaving Albridge on an up-note and pleased that he would have happy memories of his final moments with the team. He felt rather touched when, after the final whistle blew, his name was mentioned over the loudspeakers and he received appreciative cheers and applause from both fans and his team-mates for his efforts.

He entered the changing rooms as exhausted as he usually was after a match, the cold, exposed skin of his legs stinging as it was hit by the heat. His body ached, not just from the exercise it had been given over the last eighty minutes, but from the pummelling it had taken having other men slamming into it.

Guy found a spare space on a bench and began stripping off, checking himself for bruises, sometimes finding a tender, painful part to massage with his fingertips. The changing rooms were noisy with the boisterous, booming voices of men chatting, shouting and joking with each other, ebullient after the excitement of the match. The air was thick with heated bodies and it stank with a mixture of old and fresh sweat. Guy was used to the smell. It was one he always found arousing, bringing the masculinity of men directly to his nostrils as if they were as close to him as lovers. He looked around at his team-mates as they took off their kit. All the men were physically imposing in some manner as was required of the game, whether in height, muscle, weight or some combination of the three. Guy loved a big man. There was something brutish and unmistakeably manly about a guy with a beefy body that simply took his breath away and some of the men on the Albridge team had been doing exactly that to him for quite some time. He began to feel rather despondent that he would never see Mac Stevenson's broad, developed shoulders again, never look upon Jamie Carver's chunky, slightly mud-stained thighs or gaze at Matt Gillen's big chest glistening with sweat. It was a shame that he had never got closer to any of the men who surrounded him. He had found himself attracted to them many times before, but right then as they unveiled themselves of their damp and dirty kit, they appeared more beautiful than they ever had.

"Sad to be leaving us, then?" Griff Haigh, Albridge's young left wing broke Guy's drifting thoughts. He stood completely naked in front of Guy, over six-foot tall even without boots. His skin was a pale colour and his body, although not as exaggerated as some of the men around, was fit and tantalisingly shaped. Haigh was a handsome man whose movie-star looks had not yet been damaged by his time on the pitch. He had dark hair in a messy quiff. His fingernails made a rasping noise as he unconsciously scratched at his crotch causing his genitals to dance in a delightful manner.

"You're not wrong." Guy pulled off a thick sock. "There's one hell of a lot of things about this club that I'll miss."

"Well, all the jokes aside," Griff stood with his hands on his hips, then looked downwards as if embarrassed. "You know we're going to miss you as well."

He leant over and grasped Guy's shoulder firmly. "I'll miss you, Guy. I wish you the best of luck."

Guy looked up into Griff's now unflinching stare. His touch was firm but tender and his eyes friendly and, if Guy saw correctly, a little bit yearning. Guy felt very affected by the gesture. Such displays of emotion were rare in the masculine atmosphere they were in at that moment. He also felt somewhat aroused, having such a gorgeous male so near to him. Then, the instant passed as Griff's hand made a quick, flicking movement across Guy's cheek.

"I'll catch you in the bath," he said, jogging off to get clean.

"I bloody hope that's not all you'll do," Guy thought as he quickly whipped off his shorts.

Guy's last bath with his Albridge team-mates was as playful as ever. The white-tiled room that enclosed the large bath echoed with the sound of deep manly voices singing saucy chants, telling dirty jokes and poking fun at each other. The men wrestled with each other in the water: more than once Guy found himself being picked up by Bryan in a big bear hug, their naked bodies rubbing together, as Bryan's big strong arms and large firm belly trapped him before letting him fly into the water. As official 'traitor' to Albridge, Guy found himself the centre of attention, splashed, play-punched, and having the mickey taken out of him relentlessly. It was the kind of behaviour that he would miss immensely – horseplay that brought the men together, that defined and delineated their relationships with each other. And fun though it was, Guy also began to feel slightly sad. He knew that, after that day, things would never be the same. Though he was sure that he would never lose touch with the men, they would never again share the same moments of togetherness. Knowing this to be true, he subconsciously decided to make this bath time last as long as it possibly could. So, as most of the men left to dry off and dress, only Guy and two other of his team-mates remained in the bath. "I'll leave you guys to it." Guy watched as Jamie Carver climbed out of the Bath, his huge behind on unashamed display, wet and glistening. "I can hear a pint calling," Carver laughed, winking as he left the room.

Now on their own, Guy and Griff Haigh looked at each other, smiling.

"So, this is it, then," Guy leant back and stretched out his arms along the side of the bath. "Last game with Albridge finally over. I can barely believe that I'm moving on."

"Hey, don't looks so sad," Haigh said sympathetically. "It's a fantastic opportunity. Any of us would do the same thing if we got the chance. Jokes aside, I think even Bryan would."

"Yeah, I know. Deep down, I know I made the right choice. But that doesn't mean that I don't feel sad about it."

Guy gave a forced smile and then flicked his eyes suddenly downwards with despondency.

Haigh stood up, and waded over. His body looked fantastic as the water poured off it. Large, toned and damp, his sizable cock and balls jiggled against his thighs at eye-level. He sat down again right next to Guy and in an unaffected gesture of support, wrapped a meaty arm around Guy's shoulders.

"Mark my words, Guy," Haigh squeezed him heartily and Guy could feel his friend's hairy armpit rub against this skin. "You'll make us proud."

Next to such a beautiful specimen of masculinity, Guy felt the familiar warmth of attraction. Naked in the water next to a hard, hot body made the butterflies in his stomach begin to dance. Although he felt sure that Haigh's attentions were nothing more than friendly support, he couldn't help but enjoy them on another level and he quickly began to feel a lot better.

"It's just the change give me the jitters, I guess," he grinned at Haigh, this time putting more into his expression than he had done before. He took a moment to look closely at Haigh's face. He was striking, handsome, not in a plastic, TV-presenter way, but with features that had depth and character and that gave him a roguish quality. It was a face to get lost in and, at that moment, their bodies close together, their thighs rubbing against each other, it was all that Guy could do to stop himself from kissing it.

Somewhat to his surprise, Haigh never flinched once under his stare. Instead, the look was reciprocated with a friendly, open expression, until at last Haigh looked away, his attention suddenly drawn to Guy's neck.

"He's not even clean properly," he said in a mock-motherly manner. He reached over to a bottle of shower gel, squeezed some into his hand, began rubbing at the mud on Guy's neck and then gripped and tugged gently at his aching shoulders. His touch felt tender but hard and Guy couldn't help but become aroused.

"That's nice," he said. "That's just what I need right now."

"Move over here." Haigh directed him over with a quick movement of his head. "I'll give you a proper massage if you like."

Haigh positioned himself, spreading his hefty legs wide so that Guy could sit in between them. Guy felt suddenly unsure of the situation. He didn't know if it was a joke, a come-on or merely a matey offer of help. Then, deciding that, whatever was behind it, it was too good an opportunity to miss, he moved over and sat between Haigh's legs. He pushed himself backwards so that Haigh's crotch pressed against his buttocks and lower back. He sensed no erection, but the warmth and touch of the man's body around him was so fantastic his heart began to beat faster. He felt big strong hands take hold of his aching shoulder muscles and begin to knead them, hard but tenderly.

"Oh, that feels so good," Guy moaned. He began to feel incredibly relaxed under the manly caresses of his friend. He leaned forwards so that Haigh could work on it his neck and upper back. For a few moments, his eyes closed in pleasure, and then, realising the effect Haigh's touch was having on his body, he looked downwards into the water, and saw his now semi-erect penis floating upwards between his legs.

"How are your legs, mate?" Haigh asked. He now held Guy by the waist as if he was ready to move around and down. Guy suddenly became nervous again. Could he risk being caught in such a state by his team-mates?

"Er… they're okay," he said unconvincingly.

"Oh, come on, Guy." Haigh reached around anyway and began grabbing at Guy's thighs. "You'll feel a lot better for it in the morning."

There was nothing else Guy could do except enjoy Haigh's touches. He squirmed at first, Haigh's muscled arms reaching around his body, his hands grasping him and squeezing his legs, working the knees and then gradually getting higher and higher, reaching up to the inner thigh. The massage was so good that he couldn't say no, so relaxed and hoped that Haigh's hands wouldn't end up in the wrong place.

Before long, the inevitable happened… Haigh was working on a particularly sore part of Guy's upper leg, when his fingers moved too far inwards and brushed against Guy's penis. It was now fully erect and Guy felt it bouncing in the water at the accidental touch.

He quickly turned around, feeling ashamed, and started to move away.

"I'm sorry..." he began but, to his surprise, found Haigh beaming at him.

"Sit back down!" Haigh laughed. "It's the effect of the water and the massage. Don't worry, it's happened to me before as well."

Guy eyed him warily for a moment, then repositioned himself between his friend's legs.

"First game I had for Hadfield..." Haigh continued as he returned to fondling Guy's body, "... I strained my groin kicking a try. I was in a lot of pain, and I had to go and see the physio to sort it out. He got his hands right between my legs, next to my balls. He was using a lot of oils to massage me and that combined with the sensation of being touched in such a sensitive place... Well, let's just say nature took its course. I was embarrassed at first, but the physio knew exactly what to do to put me at ease."

"And what was that?" Guy asked, beginning to relax.

"He taught me how to give a proper massage," Haigh whispered quietly into Guy's ear.

"And how exactly do you give a proper massage?" Guy had already guessed the answer.

Suddenly, Haigh took hold of Guy's cock and balls gave them a good squeeze.

"Like this," he said, as he began to pull at the erection.

Guy shuddered as he felt Haigh's hands upon him, the intense pleasure of having his hard prick tugged at, his foreskin rolled over and up and back over the bulbous head, his balls tickled and jiggled. The touch felt like the culmination of the past fifteen minutes, of what having a man wrapped around him in such a manner could have only led to. He was very aroused and aching for it, but at the same time was worried at being caught out by the rest of the Albridge players.

"What if somebody comes in?" he murmured, as Haigh began to kiss his neck.

"As if. They'll be much more interested in what's happening in the pub than what's happening in here," Haigh reassured him.

Guy wasn't completely convinced, but the extra thrill of being discovered made him continue. He began rubbing his hands down Haigh's large thighs as he was masturbated, tracing the thick, defined muscles as Haigh had done his own. Haigh had a light sheen of hair on his legs that bristled against Guy's fingers as his hands moved up and down. Guy put his hands upon Haigh's chunky forearms, loving how they felt around his body, then slipped his hand downwards to Haigh's broad-fingered hands to sense how they moved upon his own genitals.

"You're quite a practitioner," he groaned. "At this kind of massage, I mean."

"I've got my own set of tools to practise on," Haigh replied, rubbing his crotch forward.

Guy realised that Haigh now had a sizable erection of his own and he could feel the thick, hard, hot member throbbing at his back. He reached behind and grabbed hold of it. It filled his grasp well. He gave it a couple of gentle wanks and Haigh moaned in appreciation. Guy moved his hand downwards in between Haigh's legs to grab hold of his friend's balls. Loosened in the warm water, the skin of Haigh's testicles floated freely on his fingers. They were more or less hairless, though Guy could feel significantly hairy patches at the sides and at the base of Haigh's cock. He reached back with his other hand and took Haigh's entire packet within his grasp, pulling at the man's bollocks and dick at the same time he himself was played with.

"I've been waiting for you to do something like that to me for a long time," Haigh whispered.

"Really?" Guy was genuinely surprised. "Well, I'm sure I can think of doing something even more pleasurable to you."

He turned around. "Ease yourself up onto the side," he told his friend. Haigh lifted himself out of the water and sat on the side, splaying his legs so that his dick and balls were fully displayed.

They glistened beautifully with droplets of water. Guy moved in closer. He began kissing Haigh at the inside of one knee, then slowly worked his way inwards until he reached the hairy patch at the crevice between Haigh's leg and his groin. He licked up it slowly, then moved onto Haigh's balls, pecking at them softly at first, before taking them in turn into his mouth and sucking on them gently.

Haigh let out a gleeful "Mmmm" at Guy's caresses, then took a sharp in-breath as Guy swiftly ran his tongue up his turgid length. The thing was not only dampened by water, but also by Haigh's sexual juices. Guy steadied the tool in his hand so he could examine it closer. It was about seven inches in length and was straight with no curves or bumps, seeming as chiselled and attractive as the rest of Haigh's body. The head had been circumcised and was round and bright pink like some rare delicious fruit. The cock was proud, and fought against Guy's grasp a couple of times with some hearty throbs. A glistening drop of pre-come decorated the piss-slit; Guy darted in with the tip of his tongue to taste it. It was warm and flavoursome and an arc of fluid suddenly conjoined the two men from penis to mouth. Guy wiped down his chin and swallowed heartily before opening his lips wide to take in Haigh properly. The meat was hot against his tongue and cheeks as he took his first suck on it, pushing his head downwards to engulf as much of Haigh as he could manage. He drew back, then moved down again, repeating the action to build up a decent steady speed. At the same time, he tickled Haigh's balls and wanked himself off, enjoying the sensation of eating another man's genitals.

Haigh placed a hand on Guy's head, gently guiding him up and down his pole, making distracted, eager grunts at every move inwards. Haigh raised himself up a little and Guy felt him begin to move his hips back and forth, softly fucking Guy's mouth. He found the change in tactic deliciously rude and felt incredibly aroused at being a receptacle for such a gorgeous man. Sometimes Haigh would pull back too far and his dick would slip out of Guy's lips with a wet smack, slapping against his belly, so that both men would fight excitedly to replace it. Eventually, however, Guy wanted the sensation of Haigh's cock somewhere else upon his body. He stood up, placing himself in between Haigh's legs once more, then turned around and bent over. He lowered himself until he felt Haigh's erection against his backside, then began writhing against it, making sure that the pressure of his skin against Haigh's own was at a level to provide maximum pleasure. He felt the thing slip between the cheeks of his arse. It felt delightful up there, steely and hot, and he forced it to slide up and down him until he was ready, more than ready for the next stage.

"I want it inside me," Guy said, turning around once more.

"I thought you'd never ask," Haigh acquiesced, pulling his friend close to him. The two men kissed ferociously, the tongues fighting over each other and into each other's mouths with abandon. They grasped huge handfuls of each other's bodies, Haigh wrapping his legs around Guy and squeezing him in tightly, Guy's dick squirming and pulsating against Haigh's belly. Guy never wanted it to end, but Haigh pulled away, standing up and wrapping a towel around himself.

"I'll be back in a minute," he said and rushed off back into the changing room. He returned quickly with a couple of packets in his hand. He dropped his towel quickly, his still-erect dick bouncing in its sudden freedom, then ripped the shiny packet open carefully. He rolled the rubber onto himself, as Guy lubed up, sticking his gunky fingers up his rectum to loosen it a little. Both men were panting with desperate fervour as Haigh slipped back into the water, standing behind Guy who now propped himself up against the side of the bath, spreading his legs to give maximum access to his entranceway. Guy gasped as he felt Haigh's prick easing up him, then shivered as it exited him once more. Soon,

Haigh was fucking him with strong, regular strokes and he bounced back to meet his buddy's every shunt. It felt as if Haigh's hands were all over him as the hard thing pumped him again and again. Eventually, he felt fingers at his crotch once more and knew that he didn't have it in him to last much longer.

"I'm nearly there," he warned.

"Me too," his friend replied.

Guy felt the shunts up him increase in ferocity, until he reached a point where he just couldn't take it anymore. He shot as Haigh wanked at him, his body racking and bucking with pleasure, his rectal muscles gripping the cock inside them again and again. A grunt at his shoulder told him that Haigh was coming too and the man on top of him embraced him tightly as his final few ruts rammed home. Guy leaned his head back so that Haigh could kiss him as both their orgasms lessened, then, after a few moments of trying to get his breath back, turned so they could embrace fully.

"Now, that's what I call a farewell present," Guy panted, utterly spent.

Three

"So, this is it." Hugo shrugged with a half-smile, then took another drag on his cigarette.

"Don't sound so final," Guy scowled at him as he placed the last box in the boot of his car. "I'll be back before you know it."

Guy had already said goodbye to his parents earlier that day, and all his friends, but he had deliberately saved Hugo for last.

"Yeah, I know." Hugo sounded far from enthusiastic, but whether it was from regret that Guy would be absent or that he would be returning, Guy was unable to tell.

"And you can always visit me!" Guy joked, trying to make the situation a little easier.

"That'll be the day," Hugo laughed. "Moi, 'oop north'? Somehow I don't think so."

Guy groaned, shaking his head. "And who said we live in a classless society?" He shut the boot and moved to take hold of Hugo.

"Come here, you upper-class twit!" he said as he took Hugo into his embrace. "I'm going to miss you."

It was true enough. He would miss Hugo. They had had some good times together. Hugo could really be a fun person to be around, when he was in the right mood, plus the fact that he was incredibly attractive and the sex they had had together had more often than not been absolutely fantastic. But, more than anything at that moment, feeling Hugo in his arms, Guy was struck by the recent memory of having another man there and the joy that it had brought him.

He was fully aware of the changes that had occurred in his and Hugo's relationship over the past few months. The coming move to Welby and the time he had spent with Griff Haigh had all accentuated their growing estrangement and he felt gravely unsure of where his future with Hugo lay. Hugo's characteristic aloofness wasn't helping matters much, either.

"But of course!" Hugo reassured Guy. And then, just a little bit too late, he added. "And I'll miss you. You're too handsome a man not to have around."

Guy got in the car. He wound down the window, feeling annoyed at Hugo's shallow, throwaway goodbye.

"I'll call you later," he smiled, then started the car and drove off.

He felt unsettled as he watched his boyfriend grow small in the rear-view mirror. He was unable to tell whether Hugo had ever really cared about him or whether his stand-offishness was merely a front and he was actually very upset that Guy was leaving London. He decided not to worry about it too much. Both time and distance would be between them now, giving them the breathing space that he felt their relationship required. Who knew what the future held for the both of them? It was impossible to tell. And besides, Guy would have a lot on his plate over the next couple of days. There was the move and all his possessions that he would have to sort out. And more than that, he had a new job, an exciting one, one that he intended to fully throw himself into. There was no time to get distracted by Hugo's inscrutability. He'd just be too busy.

Guy spent the next couple of days sorting out his new flat. The first day was the most enjoyable. One of the removal men was particularly hunky and helpful and his muscular body flexed and swelled delightfully under his tight black T-shirt as he moved Guy's furniture around. Guy couldn't help but notice that the man's smiles were bright and his behaviour very attentive and he reciprocated the interest accordingly. Surrounded by others, and with the actual task of moving at hand, nothing major happened, however. It was busy, but largely dull work after the removal men had gone and the second day was filled with unpacking boxes, sorting out ornaments, putting books on shelves, and so on. Guy liked his new flat. It was spacious and the rent was one hell of a lot cheaper than anywhere he'd lived in London. The lounge had a large window that provided a spectacular view of Welby and the rolling green hills that lay between the town and the next one. It was not long before Guy felt he could really make the place his own. And yet, on his own, so far away from friends and family, he began to feel a little lonely and became eager for the impending introduction to his new club.

It had been arranged that he should meet Ron Lambert at the club's stadium that Thursday morning. Guy woke that day, feeling nervous but excited. He showered, breakfasted and dressed casually before setting off. The journey would require a short drive across town and it would be his first chance to fully take in his new surroundings. His flat was not actually far from the town centre and it had all the usual trappings of centrally located accommodation. The block had been newly built, converted from an old warehouse and its immediate area was surrounded with similar buildings, large, old and rather striking.

Driving away from the neighbourhood, the differences between Welby and London were immediately. Welby was a town with an industrial background and as such it looked practical and functional. There had been little money in the area since the old primary trade of mining had all but disappeared less than a decade earlier and it showed. The centre was far from picturesque. The high street was dotted with shops that were empty or occupied by short-lease, clearance-style outfits. The town's focus, as far as Guy could tell, was a small shopping centre that looked rather more dilapidated than the ones he was used to, being little more than a venue for the town's medium-sized supermarket. Fortunately, Guy had never been that big on shopping. That had been more Hugo's forte. It wasn't the absence of big-name shops that made him feel slightly disappointed, but more the general grimness that struck him as he drove along. Never one to form quick impressions, however, especially ones based merely upon appearance, Guy put his lowered spirits down to the grey skies and drizzle that were imposing themselves upon the morning.

It didn't take long for him to reach the stadium. That was another thing that surprised him, being used to the traffic jams and nightmare roads of the capital city. He felt suddenly more aware of the small size of his new home. Welby could fit several times into London. It was much more like a London borough than a self-contained town. As he parked his car and got out, Guy self-consciously chose not feel claustrophobic, deciding rather to face the challenge of living somewhere so dissimilar to where he was used to.

He turned as he heard a deep voice shout his name. "Guy, over here, son."

It was Ron Lambert, walking out of the stadium's entrance. The collar was up on his thick tweed overcoat to keep out the rain and he beamed happily as Guy approached.

"You found us all right?" Lambert thrust out one of his large hands and Guy accepted it warmly.

"Yeah, I had no problem. The directions you gave me were fine."

"Welby's not a big enough place to get lost in, is it?" Lambert laughed. "I said it'd be nothing like London." Guy smiled.

"So what do you think of it from the outside?" Lambert continued, waving an arm to direct Guy's attention to the stadium. The building was large and red-brick like much of Welby. It looked old. Guy placed it somewhere around the 1930s and some of the signs looked as if they might well have been the originals. The place definitely had history and not a little charm. Guy imagined the generations of fans who had come to the stadium over the years and the emotions that it had inspired in them. Anticipation and elation, disappointment and despair seemed to seep out of the very walls of the building, ghost feelings of the many who had passed through the stadium's gates. Guy became aware that he was about to become part of that very history and hoped that he would be capable of meeting what would be demanded of him.

"It's not much from the outside," Lambert shrugged. "But just you wait till we get you in."

"Oh, I don't know," Guy said as Lambert opened the door to the entranceway. "It's certainly got something."

Lambert became quite enthusiastic as he led Guy down the corridors of the stadium. He obviously loved Welby a lot and was genuinely thrilled at having Guy joining them as a new player. Guy couldn't help but be swept up by his new boss's passion and his earlier feelings of trepidation all but disappeared. Welby's ground was impressive, too.

"And this is the exercise room," Lambert stood, hands on hips, as Guy took a look around. The room was filled with every piece of exercise equipment Guy could imagine – weights, treadmills, bikes – and it all looked new. There had been nothing like it at Albridge. If the players wanted to train there, it was simple exercise on the pitch. Or if they did want to build up a bit of muscle, they had to use a local gym and pay for it for themselves.

"I can certainly see the difference between League and Union!" Guy joked.

"Damn right there's a difference! Rugby is one of the few things that actually brings money into this town." Lambert boomed between laughs. "I suspect the change will all be quite a shock to the system at first. Come on, let me take you next door."

Lambert's voice began to echo as they entered the white-tiled space of the changing room. Even this looked somehow newer and better equipped than the ones Guy was used to.

"We had it replaced last year. New plumbing, showers, the lot. There's a sauna down the back if you've got any aches and pains. I use it every once in a while. I'll tell you what, you feel one helluva lot better afterwards."

Guy's mind wandered for a second, suddenly taken by the thought of Lambert in the sauna, a big, handsome man wearing nothing but a towel, sweating and red-faced. Guy hoped that one day they would bump into each other in there.

"Aye, aye!" Guy's daydreaming was interrupted by the opening of the door in the far corner. "You're eager, aren't you? You're not due in until tomorrow," Lambert told the man walking towards them.

He waved a small black device at them. "Forgot my mobile, didn't I?"

"You'd forget your head if it wasn't screwed on!" Lambert teased. "Guy, I'd like you to meet Alan Jones. He's our physiotherapist. You'll be seeing a lot of him."

Guy took hold of Alan's hand. Alan seemed to be in his mid-twenties. He was blond and his body was slight, but appeared fit, like a lean young footballer. He wore shiny tracksuit bottoms and a polo-neck T-shirt, the arms of which fit snugly around his nicely round biceps. He wasn't good-looking in a traditional sense, but his face was appealing and masculine, with bright eyes and a couple of days' stubble that worked to increase his attractiveness.

"I hope so!" Guy said, warmly.

"Same here," Alan nodded.

"Well, I'm glad you've met someone else around here," Lambert said. "It's a bit of a ghost town here today. I should have realised and arranged for you to meet a couple of the players."

"Don't worry about it, Ron," Guy reassured his boss. "Anyway, what's next on the agenda?"

"VIP box. Care to join us, Alan?"

"I'd love to but I'm taking my car in for a service." Alan looked genuinely disappointed.

"Oh well, another time perhaps?" Guy asked.

"Sure. I'll walk with you a little of the way, though, before I get off."

Guy let Alan take the lead, watching his pert buttocks move softly under the rustling material of his tracksuit bottoms. "And that's something that I'd love to see," he thought to himself.

"Here we are then, son." Lambert opened the door to the VIP lounge. "This is where we do our entertaining."

Guy entered the room. It was large and, though rather traditional-looking for Guy's tastes, with its oak-panelled walls and leather Chesterfields, was classically stylish in the manner of an old gentlemen's club. Like the other places Guy had been shown around, the room looked newly refurbished.

"Not bad at all," he said, running his hand along a nearby settee. "I bet you see some faces passing through here."

"You're not wrong there," Lambert nodded. He name-dropped a famous comedian who was born locally and an indie band who were from around the area. "Oh yes, they all pay us a visit when they're in town."

Lambert walked over to the room's well-stocked bar. "Hey, Guy, come get a load of this."

On the wall was a selection of photos, some black and white, showing different moments from the club's history. Guy picked out a picture of the stadium being built and several of various players, mid-game. He took a closer look at one of the group photos, showing the team lined up on the pitch, standing proud with a recently won trophy. He looked closer at the date.

"Nineteen seventy-nine," he murmured, lost in thought. "The classic line-up. That team was legendary."

"Why, thanks!" Lambert said, proudly.

Guy felt puzzled at Lambert's extreme reaction then, realising his error, examined some of the faces again. Sure enough, there was one that was a lot more familiar than the rest.

"Of course!" he said, "You played in that team!"

"Aye," said Lambert. "I'm twenty-one in that picture, believe it or not."

Lambert's young face stared back at Guy. It had all the attractive, manly qualities that it had now just over a decade later, though it was obviously somewhat fresher.

"Good-looking fellah," Guy complimented, feeling rather aroused by the young Lambert's thick, strong neck and meaty, powerful shoulders.

"Thanks kindly!" Lambert laughed and then his voice became poignant. "Best days of my life, they were. The things me and Yorkie Skelton used to get up to."

"Which one's he?" Guy asked.

Lambert pointed at a huge slab of a man, with a black eye and rough-looking, though undeniably attractive, features.

"Best loose-head prop this team's ever had. And one helluva bloke. I certainly miss having him around. You need a buddy like that when you're a young 'un. You know, someone you can get on with, someone who's on your wavelength."

"I can only imagine what you two did together." Guy had a fleeting suspicion that there was something more between Lambert and Skelton than mere friendship: Lambert seemed so wistful in his reminiscing. "What happened? To Yorkie, I mean?"

"Oh." Lambert came back down to earth with a crash. "He got a job in advertising, of all things. He's quite a name in some big company nowadays."

"Not just a pretty face, then?" Guy quipped.

Lambert chuckled. "He wasn't pretty, that's for sure. But he still had that charm about him, you know. Plenty said he was irresistible."

"See much of him now?" Guy wanted to know more.

"No, not really." Lambert sighed. "Go out for a drink every now and again if our paths cross. You know, there was a time when I thought he'd never leave." Lambert paused, before clarifying. "The game, I mean. I don't think a man like that can really do what he's doing with his life. When I do see him I get the sense that he's still yearning for it, wanting to come back. And he's not so old, neither of us are..."

"To regain what you've lost?" Guy interrupted.

Lambert thought for a second. "Aye. Something like that. Too late for me, of course."

Guy cocked his head quizzically.

"Knee injury." Lambert rubbed his left leg. "But at least I've kept my hand in. Not gone against what I know is true to me."

"And you're as good a manager as you were a player." Guy had become suddenly very sympathetic.

"Maybe." Lambert at last turned from the picture. "Anyway, enough of my sob stories. You've got it all ahead of you, my man." He walked over to the large window that took up one wall of the room. "This is what this place is all about." He spread his arms wide. "Best view of the game money can buy."

Guy moved over to join him. It was definitely quite a sight. The room offered a complete vista of the pitch and of much of the stadium itself. Once more, Guy felt possessed by the past: the stadium's striking architecture, the photographs and Lambert's stories and now this, his first outlook onto the arena that provided a home for Welby's game. It was a very imposing moment. Guy imagined himself running out onto the grass with his team-mates to the cheers of surrounding fans. He momentarily felt anxious, doubting whether he had it in him to live up to the hopes of such a demanding audience, questioning how he dare place himself in an organisation with such a fantastic and admired pedigree. But his worries quickly gave way to excitement. He could barely believe his luck to be in such a position, and couldn't wait to be given the chance to prove himself.

"You'll be fine, son," Lambert took Guy's shoulder in a hefty grip. He had obviously picked up on Guy's nerves.

Guy relaxed. With a friend like Lambert on his side, he was sure he would be.

The next week or so passed quickly, if a little strangely for Guy. In the main, he was occupied by the process of settling into his unfamiliar surroundings. He spent a day wandering through town, not looking for anything specifically, just trying to acquaint himself with the basic geography of the centre. Welby certainly was different from anywhere he had lived before. The relative lack of money in the area, compared to either London or where his parents lived, was strongly evident. With his comfortable economic background, the town seemed a little shabby and worse for wear. There were no trendy, expensive clothes shops in Welby, no ultra-modern art museums. Instead of the usual café-bars he'd frequented to get himself a latte, Guy found himself in a greasy spoon, sipping a mug of tea. But none of this seemed too much of a problem. Some of the shops and businesses he came across that day were family establishments that had been in the town for years and he was glad to see them still going and was greatly warmed by the feeling of history. What Welby lacked in facilities and modern urbanity, it made up for in real personality. Still, seemingly being the only person around with a southern accent did make him feel somewhat of an outsider. This, coupled with the fact that he was so far from family and friends, caused him to feel a little lonely in those first few days.

Unsurprisingly, then, he was delighted when the first day of pre-season training came around, being very eager to meet his team-mates and make some new buddies. The weather was a lot fresher and brighter that morning than it had been since his arrival, and he got to the ground feeling rejuvenated. He entered the locker room, large sports bag in hand, finding many of the players were already there and changing.

"Here he is!" Guy heard a familiar voice over the general rumble of the men and the clatter of boots on the tiled floor. "Our new addition to the team and one helluva fly half. Fellahs, I'd like you to meet Guy Holbrook."

It was Ron. He waved Guy into the room. "Come on, Guy, let me do some quick introductions before we start."

The atmosphere seemed a little cold to Guy, but maybe he was just feeling nervous.

"This is Jimmy Reeves, our coach."

Guy greeted Jimmy with a smile, before he was quickly moved on.

The next person Lambert introduced Guy to seemed more interested in the contents of his sports bag than in speaking to his new team-mate. "'Gripper' Mason. Solid forward. Good man."

Mason was bent over with his back to Guy, until Guy stuck his hand out in greeting. Mason then stood up, showing off his size fully. Appropriate to the position he played, he was a massively-built man. Guy estimated him to be a good six-foot-five and inwardly joked to himself that his shoulders seemed to be almost as wide. Without saying a word, Mason took hold of Guy's hand. The squeeze was a strong one that all but took the amiable expression off Guy's face. He was beginning to wonder whether it was some kind of a test on Mason's part, when Mason released him and returned his attentions to his bag.

"I can see why they call you 'Gripper'," Guy chuckled. Mason made a grunting noise that Guy supposed might have been a laugh.

"He doesn't say much, our Grip," Lambert interjected. "But you just see what he can do on the pitch."

Lambert moved on again. Guy felt a little dejected at Gripper's reaction, but remained determined to make a good impression on the rest of the men. Unfortunately, he didn't seem to fare that much better with the majority of them, who either seemed to regard their encounter with some detachment, or even with a little hostility. There were only a couple who seemed at all friendly. Thankfully, one of them, Kyle Taylor, was enthusiastic at meeting him, having seen him play a couple of times.

Guy put his bag down next to Kyle's so he could get to know him better, but before he began changing, he decided to make another attempt at getting into his team-mates' good books.

"Okay, fellahs! Just a quick word," he shouted, bringing the room to silence. "Nothing major. No speech or anything. I'd just like to say how glad I am to meet you all and how excited I am at being on the team. I think we'll all get along just fine and I can see this next season being one of the best."

A mocking voice interrupted him: "Oh, he's *sooo* glad to meet us and *sooo* excited at being on the team! How la-di-dah!" It was Georgie Grant, Welby's scrum half, trying to bring off an upper-class accent. He got a couple of laughs and, rather than having the desired effect, the men simply returned to putting on their kit, and Guy found himself ignored.

"Can it next time, Grant!" Lambert, who had been looking on, snarled. "Thanks, Guy. I'm sure we all appreciate your words and are as happy to have you here as you are to be here. Now, lads, get a move on. I want you outside in ten minutes."

Guy's spirits fell. He had tried to laugh off Grant's teasing with the other men. He knew how all-male atmospheres were prone to pranks and mickey-taking and that the only way not lose face was to take such punches on the chin. But was there something more behind what Grant had said? Some genuine animosity, perhaps? And were his team-mates merely being reserved, or were they less than keen to have him around? He felt unsure and yet didn't want to give in to negativity on his first real day at the club.

"Don't give it a second thought." Kyle broke Guy's ponderings, pulling up his shorts at the same time. "What Grant said, I mean. He'd be far happier if you'd burped in his face than if you showed you wanted to be his friend."

Guy laughed. "Thanks, Kyle." He watched as Kyle tugged off his shirt, revealing a well-toned set of pectorals and stomach muscles. His chest had a splash of hair that just invited the caress of fingers. Suddenly aroused, Guy took a quick look around him. The room was filled with thick thighs and broad shoulders, skin fully exposed or half dressed in sports gear. Some of the Welby men weren't half bad-looking at all; others were rougher but still attractive, with their rugby-beaten faces oozing masculinity. Guy felt cheered at the sight. Maybe things at Welby wouldn't be so bad after all.

Outside, the training began with some simple warm-ups and stretching exercises, which led onto some straightforward circuits to get the blood circulating. As a coach, he found Jimmy demanding but not unapproachable and he was glad that the man treated him in the same way he treated the other men, neither more favourably nor any worse. He could feel himself settling in more with a physical task at hand and, though he wasn't in a position to speak much with his team-mates, felt a little bit closer to them as a result of their shared task. It wasn't long before Guy noticed just how fit the team was. Much fitter than him, in fact. Despite his being in good shape, with his time at Albridge and a couple of trips to the gym a week to keep him healthy, the others had a noticeable edge and he found himself panting and sweating more than them and becoming tired more quickly. Of course, he knew the reason why. Welby, as a full-time, professional team, had been working on a more intensive fitness scheme than Albridge. Although Albridge met to practise regularly, the fitness of individual players was more or less up to them. Many men on the team had little or no exercise outside the game, relying on skill and often physical size to make an impression on the pitch. Guy knew one player whose idea of exercise amounted to little more than numerous pints of beer to maintain his sizeable belly. This being the case, Guy quickly began to feel out of his depth. By the time the team moved onto some passing exercises, he was halfway to exhaustion and his weariness had been perceived by those around him, too. He was wiping the sweat off his brow with his sleeve when he felt a hand on his shoulder.

"Word in your ear, son." It was Jimmy Reeves. "Do you want to take five minutes? Pretend you've gone for a piss, or summat."

Unfortunately for Guy the conversation was overheard.

"Don't worry about him, Reevesy," Georgie Grant jogged by, chuckling with malice. "Union boy, isn't he? And a southerner. Can't take the pace."

"I'll show you pace in a minute, Grant," Reeves warned.

Determined not to lose face, Guy decided to stick around.

"I'll be all right, Jim," he panted.

"Good on you," Reeves said, encouragingly. "It'll not be so hard from now on, anyway."

Guy ran off to join the rest of the men. Reeves was right. The running and passing was not so hard on his system as the circuits had been and the exercise was punctuated by many short breaks that kept his pulse rate at a lower level than before. He began to feel bolstered again and was glad to have an opportunity to show off what he could do with the ball. He seemed as talented as the other men, if not more so in some cases. Before long, his abilities were noticed and he received appreciative comments from Reeves and even from some of his team-mates.

It was only when Reeves switched to work on tackling that things really took a turn for the worse. Guy felt very tired by this point, his limbs weak and his face burning up. But once more, he decided to continue rather than take a break, thinking that the only way he would increase the punishment his body could take would be to carry on.

The task was straightforward. One man was given the ball to run with while the others, one by one, tried to bring him down. Initially, Guy did quite well, tackling a couple of his team-mates to the ground. Once again, his efforts were appreciated by some of the men around him. But when it came to his turn to run the gauntlet, things didn't go so smoothly.

Tired as he was, he knew he would have to resort to tactics and prowess rather than strength to succeed. Starting at one end of the pitch, he dodged the first couple of attacks, fooled the third, then narrowly managed to pull himself out of the clutches of the fourth. Then, before he had chance to even think about the fifth, he was hit and down and in pain. He had not seen the man coming at all. The tackle had been very hard, and he had fallen awkwardly, badly straining his ankle.

"Not too clever now, are you, Holbrook?" said Grant and Guy realised why he'd been taken down so hard.

"Bit early that, Grant, wasn't it?" Reeves joined the men as they got up off the ground. "You didn't give him a bloody chance!"

"What's up, Reevesy?" Grant snarled. "New boy taken your fancy?"

"You want to watch yourself. This game's about teamwork, not about individuals, not about petty rivalries. You're not so good a player that you won't get benched in a few weeks' time, you know that?"

Grant walked off, swearing under his breath.

"You all right, son?" Jimmy asked as Guy tried to stand on the painful foot. "That Grant's a dickhead. His anger can be good on the pitch but, when its focused on the wrong target, it's nothing but trouble."

"Yeah, I'm okay. Dealt with worse than him in my time, anyway." Guy winced as he limped around.

"Well, it doesn't look that way right now. I'm taking you off for a while. Get back inside and get Alan to give you the once over."

"I'll be fine…" Guy began. It really didn't seem that serious. Back in Union he had played with worse injuries. And besides, he didn't want it to look like he was giving in to Grant.

"Yeah, you will be. But after a rest and after we've seen to that ankle."

Realising there was little point in arguing, Guy acquiesced. It was true that, back at Albridge, he had continued to play despite having taken some far heavier knocks than this one, but he had to accept that things were done differently in League. It was a far greater risk to Welby to lose a player through a minor injury that might become aggravated in time. League players were paid to be able to play. He had been brought in with a sizeable contract, based on his having a good career ahead of him, not on his missing matches simply because of some minor incident during training. Guy couldn't help but be disappointed, however, as he walked off the pitch. It was his first day with Welby, his first real chance to prove himself and bond with his team-mates. He felt resentful at Grant for the dodgy tackle and far from happy at the way his initial steps with the rest of the team had gone.

As he entered the changing rooms, his despondency weighed on him. However, he remembered Alan's friendliness the previous week and hoped that the man would be able to work on his spirits as much as he would his ankle.

He found Alan in his room, deep in a newspaper.

"Oh, all right, Guy?" Alan stood up, and put away what he was reading. "Just having a flick through the sports pages. There's a piece on you in there, if you want a look."

He cottoned onto Guy's mood. "Hey, who's pissed on your bonfire?"

"Sorry, Alan. I've just had a bit of an accident, bit of a nasty tackle. Sprained my foot a little. I'm sure it's nothing really."

"Well, let's take a look at it. Hop on here and lie down."

The room had a centrally positioned, specially designed 'bed' for injured players to be examined on. Guy got on and lay back, propping himself up with his elbows.

"Don't worry, mate, I'll be careful," Alan smiled, as he gingerly pulled at Guy's bootlaces. Despite the physio's gentleness, Guy couldn't stop himself from cringing as Alan eased off his boot.

"Sorry. Was that painful?"

"Not too much." Guy put on a brave face.

"Just your sock now, then we can have a proper look at you."

Alan took hold of the top of Guy's thick woollen sock and gradually pulled it downwards. Despite how sore Guy's ankle felt at that moment, he couldn't help but become a little aroused at being so slowly and sensually undressed by Alan. Alan was a very attractive man. His dark-blond hair was short and a growth of dark stubble accentuated his bright eyes. His frame was slight, wiry even, but well-proportioned and it fitted his blue sports sweatshirt and black tracksuit bottoms very nicely, Guy thought. Was it mere suspicion, or was Alan taking rather a long time taking off Guy's footwear, as if relishing the moment as well?

"Ouch!" Alan took a sharp intake of breath. "It looks slightly swollen."

Guy looked down. His ankle was red and definitely a little larger than normal.

"Listen," Alan continued. "Lie back and I'll check for any major damage."

Guy did as he was told and then felt the pleasant sensation of Alan's hands upon him. The touch was firm but tender, feeling along the sole of his foot and base of his leg. He could feel his sweat cooling in the air. The moisture felt good between his skin and another man's, but he still felt a little self-conscious.

"Sorry about the smell," he apologised. "They've been working me hard out there today."

Alan laughed. "Don't worry about it, mate. Think I'm used to a little sweat by now."

At that moment, he got to what was causing the problem and Guy flinched accordingly.

"That better?" Alan squeezed Guy's leg from a totally different angle and the pain diminished significantly.

"Yeah, that's great," Guy moaned with relief.

"I see what the trouble is now," Alan said. "Nothing serious. It'll be fine by tomorrow, I should imagine. I'll just give it a quick work-over and strap it up for you."

Alan began to massage Guy carefully. "So, who did this to you, then?"

Guy sighed. "Georgie Grant," he replied. "I get the feeling he doesn't like me too much."

"Oh, he's all bark and no bite, that one. When his temper gets out of control, though..." Alan tutted. "Well, I guess it's not my place to comment on what people say about him behind his back. He's never said anything out of order to me, like. My Mum and his live on the same street and, if you think he can be a bit of a terror, you ought to see her!"

Guy chuckled.

"That's better! First smile I've seen on you since you came in here!"

His pain lessening, Guy became more and more relaxed as Alan worked on him. He realised what he needed right then was a shoulder to cry on and, feeling secure as a result of Alan's amiability, he began to open up.

"Oh, I don't know," he began. "It doesn't seem to be much of a first day so far. And it's not just Grant, I suppose, it's..."

"Go on," Alan encouraged. "I'm like a shrink. Stuff I've heard in here you wouldn't believe. Money, sex lives, car troubles, I've heard it all in here. But I'm telling you, none of it ever gets past these four walls."

Reassured, Guy began to relate how he had felt this morning, about how high his hopes were for the day, excited at the prospect of meeting new friends and starting an interesting new job. He had not exactly had his hopes dashed, but definitely quashed somewhat by the less-than-enthusiastic response to his arrival.

"I just couldn't tell whether people didn't want me around, really. Not many seemed particularly welcoming," he sighed forlornly.

Alan paused and cleared his throat before going on. "It'll be nerves, mainly. Starting a new job anywhere is hard. You've got to ease yourself in, establish yourself into a network of people that know each other already, that are pretty tight with each other. And you can't get much tighter than you do with a sports team."

"I guess not," Guy chuckled. Although Alan's brief moment of reticence had concerned him, bringing to the surface doubts whether there were other reasons he hadn't been immediately accepted by the players, he did definitely feel better for having talked about his worries.

"And northern men, mate," Alan continued, "We're a reserved set of people. Not really known for being particularly forthcoming. But once you get used to us, I think you'll find us all right."

"Well, you seem a nice enough fellah," Guy smiled.

"Thanks," Alan said warmly. He looked deep into Guy's eyes for a few seconds, making Guy wonder whether his amiability was something more than an offer of mere friendship. "Now, how's that feel?"

Alan carefully laid Guy's leg down again.

"Better, thanks," Guy felt rather disappointed that Alan's hands had moved from him.

"Anything else I can help you with?" Alan asked chirpily. "While you're in here?"

Feeling suddenly impetuous, Guy decided to take a chance on his intuition.

"Actually," he began. "There is something. An old injury that's been playing up over the past couple of days. Any chance you can check it out for me?"

"No problem." Alan moved to stand with his hands on his hips. "Where is it that's causing you the trouble?"

Guy hesitated a little, as if embarrassed, before continuing. "It's my groin."

Alan laughed, shaking his head. "No need to be shy, mate. I've seen it all before, remember. Now swing yourself round and get your shorts off, but be wary of your ankle. I've still not bound it up yet."

Guy did as he was told, first removing his remaining boot and sock, then easing his shorts downwards and off. The bottom half of his body was now totally naked and he felt aroused at being exposed like that in front of another man.

Alan stood in front of him. "Now, if you'd like to spread your legs a little wider. I need to get in there and have a good feel around."

"And that's exactly what I want you to do," Guy thought to himself. He did as he was told, splaying his thighs so that his cock and balls were fully exposed to the fresh air.

"Tell me if you feel anything twinge." Alan smiled at him as he made the first tentative touches upon Guy's thigh. The touch was warm and gentle but firm and Guy enjoyed it immensely.

"It's a bit further up, actually," Guy encouraged. He leant backwards and propped himself up with his hands on the bed. "I know it's a bit of a bind but it's right between my legs."

"No bind," grinned Alan. He slid his fingers upwards. He squeezed and rubbed the top of Guy's leg, then placed his hand right in the crevice between Guy's thigh and his balls. "How's that?" he asked.

"That's the spot, all right." Guy could feel the blood surging around his body as he became more and more excited. "Very sensitive there. Anything I can do about it?"

"I don't think it's anything serious. Probably a minor strain.

Have you tried massage at all?"

"Not really. I haven't seen anyone about it before," Guy replied innocently.

"Here. Let me show you what to do." Alan walked over to a cupboard on the wall and took out a plastic squeezy bottle. Guy gave his friend a quick once-over. He couldn't tell whether it was his imagination or not, but it did seem as if the bulge at the front of Alan's tracksuit bottoms had got larger in the past few minutes.

"Now, nothing to worry about, mate. We all know what we've got down there, don't we? And I've done this sort of thing a million times, so it doesn't bother me in the slightest." He squirted out some oil into his palm and rubbed his hands together.

"I bet you have," said Guy, as Alan replaced his fingers upon him.

"Just move you out of the way a bit, mate." With his left hand, Alan softly pressed Guy's genitals to one side so he could really get his right hand in deeply. Guy inhaled sharply at the rush of pleasure that came over him.

"Sorry," Alan said sheepishly. "Did that hurt?"

Guy put on a brave face. "It's fine," he replied. The sensation of Alan's slippery fingers sliding over him was exquisite.

"Do it like this. Firm, but not so much pressure that you hurt yourself."

"I see," Guy looked downwards. He loved to see Alan's hands upon him like that, caressing him in such a private place. He suddenly became aware that he was enjoying himself a little too much: his penis, though not fully erect, was becoming noticeably larger and filled with blood. And it was happening at the wrong moment, too.

"Now you give it a go," Alan began. "It'll help you in the long run if you can do this from time to time at home."

He moved his hands away and Guy cringed as Alan looked down.

"Sorry," he apologised. "I'm just a bit sensitive down there. Like I said."

"Don't worry about it." To Guy's relief, Alan shrugged the situation off. "I know what it's like being touched down there. I like it, too." And then, changing the subject completely, he continued. "You got a girlfriend?"

"Er... no." Guy wasn't entirely sure where Alan was heading.

"Been a long time, has it? Sex-wise, I mean."

Guy thought back to his time with Griff Haigh, then lied. "Yes, I suppose."

"Me, too," Alan eased himself onto the bed next to Guy. "Me and my lass split up last year and there hasn't really been anyone since. The nights are long without it, aren't they?"

Guy nodded. The shiny material of Alan's tracksuit bottoms brushed against his leg.

"I'll tell you what. I've seen you like that..." he nodded at Guy's prick, which lay heavy and pointing downwards, but still thickened over his balls, "... and given you a good feel. How's about you do the same for me? Just two buddies helping each other out of a bad situation." Alan winked and there was a large, friendly grin on his face. "Take your mind off your ankle, in any rate."

"All right, Alan. I don't see why not. We're both grown men, aren't we?"

Guy had got exactly what he wanted. He could feel himself salivating as Alan pulled down his tracksuit bottoms to reveal a decent-sized prick and balls. He shuffled his legs apart a little to expose himself a little more.

"Put a bit of oil on it. It'll make it feel better."

Guy reached around Alan for the bottle and, turning it upside down, gave it a squeeze so that a good blob of oil oozed out and onto Alan's member. He saw the thing twitch pleasingly as the oil fell upon it and gradually it began to increase in size.

"Go on, mate," Alan encouraged. "Don't be shy."

Guy placed his hand upon Alan, causing the man to shudder with pleasure. He traced the oil with his finger tips, then began to massage it into the growing piece. The thing was still fleshy to the touch like a piece of raw meat and yet, second by second, Guy could feel it getting more and more hard. He ran his fingers up and down the crack between Alan's legs, just as Alan had done to him, and Alan murmured an appreciative "Yes, that's it" as he did so. He took Alan's balls into his grasp and cupped them. They were hairy and large, the soft skin spilling over the side of his palm as he squeezed them. He slid his hand across Alan's thighs, enjoying the tickle of thin hairs on his hand. Alan's skin was relatively dark but not tanned and it gave him a healthy look.

By this point Alan had become fully erect and Guy took a moment to appreciate the view of him. Alan's penis was a pleasing but not overwhelming size, looking a little over six inches and nicely thick. It had a substantial foreskin that pursed at the top, allowing only a little of the deep-purple head to show through. A mighty blue vein traced its way half way up the thing before splitting into several branches that decorated the underside. Guy desperately wanted to bend over and take it into his mouth, but he restrained himself.

"Take hold of it, mate. It's not gonna bite you." Alan's cock trembled as he spoke and at last Guy took it fully in his grasp. Alan moaned as he did so.

"Nice one, mate," he mumbled. "Fucking been a long time since anyone did that, I can tell you."

Guy gave the prick a good squeeze.

"Now give it a good tug. A good wank, like you would your own."

Guy did as he was told, first pulling the loose skin up and over Alan's dick so that his foreskin bunched up at the end, then dragging it back down. He found he was able to pull it back fully so that the bulbous end could be seen completely. He repeated the motion a couple of times, feeling Alan throb against his grasp, then just tickled the end with his fingers where the oil had made it good and greasy.

"Oh, mate, that's bloody gorgeous," Alan had his eyes closed and he shook his head as if in amazement. "But you're letting me get carried away. I'm leaving you out of it, aren't I?"

Alan took hold of Guy's shoulders and moved him back a little. "Now let's sort you out as well."

Feeling incredibly aroused at that moment, Guy's prick had reached full erection and it angled up and away from his splayed thighs.

"You don't muck about, do you?" Alan laughed as he poured out more oil onto Guy. "Big lad, as well. Bet you keep the ladies pleased."

"Not quite," Guy thought to himself. He winced with pleasure as Alan began massaging him once more, firstly as before between his legs, then all over his balls, causing tingling waves of sensation over his body. He couldn't help but become aroused even further and his penis pulsated repeatedly, desperate for further stimulation.

"You like that, don't you?" Alan asked.

"Certainly do," Guy panted.

"Well, you'll like this even better," Alan said, assured as he took hold of Guy's man-meat. Guy shuddered as he felt the man pull at him while kneading his testicles. Being touched like that was one of his favourite forms of sex play. There was something so deliciously dirty about showing himself to another man like that and having someone pay so much attention to his genitals as a result. Alan was obviously enjoying it, too. Guy sensed Alan's confidence in the situation: he was being masturbated by someone with not a little sexual skill and he guessed it was not the first time Alan had performed such an act on someone else.

"How was that, then?" Alan looked at Guy with a sexy, cheeky grin.

"You definitely know your way around the body," Guy complimented.

"Comes with being a physio," Alan played with himself idly as he spoke. "Now, how's about both at the same time."

Their arms crossed over each other and they began to wank each other's parts simultaneously.

"That's it, mate," Alan encouraged. "Get in there. I really like having my bollocks felt."

Guy followed his instructions, enjoying Alan's little noises of satisfaction. The two men were very physically close and, though the occasional bumping of their arms felt a little clumsy, the situation was incredibly sexy. Both of them were panting heavily with pleasure and, every time he looked at Alan, the man smiled at him, obviously incredibly happy.

"Fucking good, isn't it?" Alan said, breathily. "Who needs a girlfriend when you've got a good mate?"

"You've got me convinced." Guy could feel the forefinger on his left hand, the one he was using on Alan, becoming a little sticky. He looked down and found that the ring of skin at the top of Alan's penis was filled with pre-come. He dipped a finger into the receptacle of warm, viscous fluid, pulled it out so that a long string of juice arced in the air, then rubbed it all over the head of Alan's cock.

"Sorry, mate," Alan muttered in between groans. "Making your fingers a bit of a mess."

"Happens to us all," Guy reassured him. "I'm going to be doing a lot worse to yours in a minute."

Seeing Alan's increased ecstasy, Guy decided to take a risk. With his other hand, he moved a little further back between Alan's thighs, past his testicles to the patch of skin that led to the crack of his backside. Although half expecting some sort of rebuttal, he was genuinely surprised when none came and Alan became more aroused still at being touched there. He pushed underneath even further, loving the sensation of hairy, secret skin upon his fingers. The crevice was warm and a little damp from sweat and he poked around to find his target. Then, there it was, a circle of wrinkled but firm skin trembling upon his middle finger. He traced round it gently and Alan began to squirm, easing himself forwards so that Guy could gain better access.

"Go on, Guy," Alan had his eyes closed now. He had stopped wanking Guy, lost in his own pleasure, but still gripped him strongly. "Give it a good tickle."

Guy rubbed the hole, then lightly flicked his finger again and again over it, before making a first, tentative attempt at an insertion. He found it extremely unyielding, as if nothing had been put up there before. He removed his hand, spat on his fingers for extra lubrication, then tried again. Alan swore as Guy managed to penetrate him.

"Never even done that to myself before," Alan moaned.

Guy was barely inside Alan at all. He found the chute squeezed his finger extremely tightly and he wiggled around a little to loosen it up.

"Do you like it, though?" Guy asked.

"It's bloody fantastic!" Alan exclaimed. "Here, let me move round. I'll do the same for you after."

He got off the bed, his hard length bouncing in the air as he did so, pulled his tracksuit bottoms down around his ankles then bent over.

"Get right up there," he said. "Try it with some oil."

Alan looked fucking amazing. His sweatshirt was rising up to reveal a lithe back and his buttocks had split nicely. His arse was hairless, though his crack wasn't, and his slim but shapely legs looked particularly inviting framed by the sportswear above and below them.

Guy squirted some more oil out into his hands, then rubbed it all over Alan's backside. Alan had a good, round, firm bum and Guy got a great thrill out of fondling it. Once more, he moved further in, greasing the warm split and making Alan's anus good and moist. This time, he found his finger slipped in much easier and he managed to get one fully inside. Alan grunted his appreciation loudly. After letting his digit settle a couple of seconds, Guy started sliding it slowly out and then in again. He repeated the motion with no protest from Alan and, regarding the minor seduction as a success, began doing it over and over again. Steadily, Alan's tunnel became slacker.

"Think you can manage another one?" Guy asked. "I find it gets better when you have at least a couple up there."

"Anything, mate," Alan replied. "Just don't stop doing what you're doing. It feels fucking brilliant."

Gently, Guy moved his forefinger alongside his middle finger and pushed in. The fit was tight, but he sensed Alan relaxing as he became used to being touched like that. Taking another chance, Guy moved closer to Alan as he started to frig his new friend. He stood so that his legs straddled one of Alan's and his thighs gripped the sides of Alan's hamstrings, his cock and balls lying upon Alan's greased behind.

"Don't mind, do you mate?" The warmth and texture of Alan's slippery skin felt wonderful on the underside of Guy's genitals.

"Your dick's so hot," Alan seemed distant, dreamy, "'s nice."

Guessing just how much Alan was enjoying his introduction to sex with another man, Guy decided to take yet another step. Aligning both movements in time, he began to ruck his hips back and forth at the same speed as he moved his fingers in and out. He shuddered at the sensation of rubbing his penis on someone else and thrilled at the fact that it was all seemingly new to Alan. Soon enough, Alan was moving backwards to meet Guy's gyrations, increasing the friction on Guy's dick and pushing himself onto Guy's fingers. They both wanted more, but to Guy's surprise, it wasn't he who moved things on further this time.

"I want to see how it feels," Alan suddenly said.

"How what feels?" Guy wanted to hear him say it.

"I need something bigger inside me. I want to see how your hot prick feels being shoved right up my arse."

"It'd be my pleasure." They quickly discussed protection and Alan revealed he kept an emergency condom in his wallet. Guy found the wallet on the bench at the side, speedily took out the small shiny packet and then carefully opened it. He rolled it onto himself as Alan, looking over his shoulder, watched with half-shut, desirous eyes.

"This is gonna be something, I can tell," he panted.

"I'll do my best." Guy was as horny as anything at the prospect of taking a straight man's cherry and his penis became harder still. Positioning himself behind Alan, he bent his knees a little to align his knob end with Alan's opening. Both of them gasped at the delightful coming-together of their bodies, then groaned simultaneously at the initial move inwards. Guy felt Alan open up around him and grasp the end of his length. There was much resistance, but he kept pushing gradually and he felt the arse slowly give more and more until finally he was fully inside. Alan was making quite a lot of noise by that point and Guy leant over him, concerned.

"Does it hurt too much?" he asked, hoping to the utmost that it didn't.

"It hurts, all right," Alan replied. "But I like it, mate. I really fucking like it."

Alan really was tight around him, and Guy felt he could've stayed in that clasping, comfortable fissure forever. However, he also wanted to show Alan the works, what it really was like to get fucked. He withdrew slightly and then returned upwards, just as he had done with his fingers previously. The action was warmly received, so he repeated the motion, giving a few slow, tentative bucks with his hips. His body shivered at being inside a virgin arse like that. He increased the speed and depth of his strokes, again unsure of what Alan could take, or would want. Once more, he was pleased when Alan seemed to be really getting off on the experience.

"Do it faster, for me, Guy," he pleaded. "I can take it. I really want to feel you fucking me fast and hard."

Never one to let so horny a request pass, Guy became more forceful and eager. He took hold of Alan's waist and dragged his buddy back onto him to meet his every upstroke. Their bodies began slapping together with a regular rhythm, Alan grunting every time Guy pushed himself fully inside. Guy started to feel the familiar rising within him. His penis was incredibly rigid, the end sensitive in the extreme. He knew what was about to happen. He leant over Alan so that his chest rubbed against Alan's back and the warmth of the man's body underneath him turned him on even more. The pleasure in his cock became more and more intense and acute. All his muscles grew tense as he screwed Alan harder and harder, his balls bouncing against Alan's backside, and he began to lose concentration. Only one thing mattered now and that was the inevitable, impending release. He thrust and thrust, the ecstasy in his body peaking. At first it focused at the end of his dick and then, as the first jet of fluid was released from him, it spread throughout his being with wave upon wave of joy. He could feel his manhood throbbing uncontrollably inside Alan as he pumped away at him, his hot sperm filling the rubber and coating him with sticky warm liquid. He cried out repeatedly and then as the pulsations within him lessened, he suddenly felt exhausted and let himself rest a moment on top of his friend.

"Feeling better?" Alan asked after Guy's hard breathing had died down a little.

"I'm feeling bloody wonderful," Guy complimented, standing

up once more.

"No," Alan warned. "Leave it inside me. It's my turn now."

Guy's cock was still rigid so he did what he was told. Alan raised the upper part of his body, pressing his back against Guy once more. Guy looked over the man's shoulder to see his engorged, expectant prick angling upwards at the hem of his sweatshirt. Alan took hold of Guy's hands, placing one on his cock and the other on his balls.

"Go on, mate," he implored. "Bring me off as well."

Wanting to see Alan aroused and hard from his touch, he began to masturbate his friend. He guessed what Alan wanted was good hearty action, so he tugged at the thing with abandon, all the while fondling Alan's balls with his other hand. It didn't take long before Alan became incredibly hot and steely to the touch and the pre-come simply poured from him. Guy felt the man stiffen in his arms and then, to his delight, Alan came hard. He watched as the white streams flew from the dick in his hand, streaking across the bed. The mess was hot and it oozed out over his fingers as the piece fought against his grasp again and again. He felt the muscles of Alan's rectum tighten then relax with every ripple of his orgasm. Gradually, the contractions decreased and Alan went lifeless in front of him. They stayed together a while. The warmth of their afterglow made Guy feel very close to Alan, and proud that he had been responsible for Alan's first gay fuck.

"Bloody fantastic," Alan said emphatically as he finally turned to face Guy.

"You're telling me," Guy said. His hands were sticky and he wiped them off on his shirt before he grabbed hold of Alan again and pulled him in close to his body. "There was one thing I missed out, though."

Alan smiled at him. He didn't struggle against Guy's arms and their embrace felt comfortable and natural. Taking his final chance on the situation, Guy kissed Alan fully on the lips. The kiss was little more than a peck at first, then it gradually became more involved and energetic and soon tongues and lips were wrestling against each other in a caring, passionate manner.

Guy was the first to pull away, wanting to see the effect his actions had had on his new friend. To his amusement, Alan was fully distracted by physical joy once more, his eyes closed, a faraway, wistful expression on his face. After a few seconds his eyes opened and he began to grin, cheeky and sexy again.

"I'll tell you what," he beamed, proud and happy. "I could get used to this."

"So could I," Guy confirmed as they cuddled. "Alan, mate, so could I."

Four

The next few weeks went more or less smoothly for Guy. Busied by the rush of change, his life seemed to move very quickly. Much of his time now was taken up by work for Welby. He trained with them at least three times a week and did some kind of other fitness work everyday.

It was difficult at first. He felt unfit and out of shape, especially compared to the others on the team. Although his ankle injury cleared up in a few days (thanks to help from Alan), there were many nights when his body ached terribly as he got into bed and, exhausted, he would immediately fall into the deepest of deep sleeps. But, as he had shown during his first training session, he had the skill to justify his being with the team and the determination to improve himself. Before long, he noticed changes in his physiological make-up. He could run for longer, dodge tackles quicker, kick the ball harder and was lifting much heavier weights in the gym. He didn't lag behind the rest of his team as much, needing as few breaks as they did, and it took much longer for him to feel red-faced and sweaty on the pitch. His body altered accordingly as well, his shoulders, chest and legs growing in size and becoming more trim and from time to time he found himself enjoying and noticing the changes in front of the mirror at home. Naked, he'd flex a bicep to check out its progress or look over his shoulder while squeezing his buttocks together. He was pleased with the progress, feeling much healthier and believing that he was in the best shape he had ever been.

His relationships with the other men at Welby did not develop so well, however. They moved as slowly as he guessed they would after his first training day. There were definitely some who warmed to him almost immediately. Ron Lambert continued to be relentless in his encouragement of him, and was obviously overjoyed to have him on board. Jimmy Reeves seemed very impressed with what Guy had to offer on the pitch and, though he pushed him hard – sometimes, Guy felt, harder than he did the others around him – Guy guessed that it was just because he could see the potential inside him and wanted the best from him.

There were a couple of players as well who were friendly to Guy, most notably Kyle Taylor, who seemed to have no qualms about the new addition to his team. In the main, though, Guy didn't feel totally accepted. Largely, his team-mates remained as stand-offish towards him as they had done that first day, usually being uninterested in him or, in the case of Georgie Grant, outright hostile on occasion. He never rose to the challenge of Grant's taunts about him being a southerner or that he had had a well-off background. He simply laughed them off, realising that to show his anger or hurt would be to show that there were chinks in his armour and that Grant was affecting him, which would cause the teasing to get worse. Despite his best efforts, there appeared to be a barrier between him and certain members of the team. Some of his worries he shrugged off as his own nerves, others he put down to the 'northern reticence' Alan had warned him about. But Guy realised that total acceptance at Welby was far from in sight and he just hoped that when the team actually started playing together for real things would change for the better.

Guy gradually began to get used to living in Welby. Although it was vastly different from anywhere he had lived before, he started to like the closeness that was integral to the town's character. Often, if he needed a paper or had run out of milk, he would pop out to the small shop that was on a street around the corner. He warmed to how the woman behind the counter greeted him with genuine interest and friendliness each time, to the point where she eventually called him by his first name. Their conversations would last several minutes, with her showing interest in the team and how his training was going, and him asking her about her daughter's impending marriage and so on. People in Welby, unlike London, had the time to take an interest in those around them, and he greatly liked this aspect of the town's character. He was still spending quite a lot of time out of the town, though. He made many trips at weekends to see his parents. He never revealed to them his concerns about how he was fitting in to the team, wanting neither to worry them nor to receive a lecture from his mother about how she had been right all along.

He also went back to London to see friends. He stayed with Hugo, although it was becoming increasingly obvious to him that they were moving further and further apart. They behaved as if they were still boyfriends and yet quickly brought each other to states of irritability. Guy found Hugo's disparaging references to Welby and the town's inhabitants as being throwbacks to another time very annoying. He found himself gritting his teeth every time Hugo made out his new job was a hobby that he would be giving up on in a couple of months. Guy seemed to rub Hugo up the wrong way as well. Hugo told him on more than one occasion that he thought Guy was changing (for the worse, of course). On one visit, despite sharing the same bed, they avoided sleeping together, Guy claiming tiredness and Hugo saying he was too drunk. The night felt extremely awkward to Guy and he became very aware that the end of their relationship was near – and perhaps inevitable. Not wanting, however, to move on from such a long-term and important relationship without giving himself time to think about it, he stopped taking trips to London for a while.

He never really felt lonely in Welby. A lot of the time he was too busy. And the few friends he had made in the town were more than happy to help him out with the spare time he did have. His best new chums were Alan and Kyle, who individually and sometimes together, took delight in showing him what Welby had to offer a young man in his prime, taking him out on the town when his strict exercise and diet regime would allow it. He found Welby's nightlife obviously a lot more toned down than London's but was rather taken by some of the local pubs, which had a comfortable, family atmosphere to them.

During the first few weeks after their initial meeting, Guy and Alan often had sex, and both of them enjoyed it and each other's company greatly. But Guy never considered Alan a potential full-time boyfriend and sensed that the free-and-easy approach to their relationship was reciprocated. Alan appeared to be a man who was just starting to blossom, to develop a new life of his own that he obviously enjoyed immensely and, though Guy knew they would remain friends, he also knew that romantically their paths went separate ways. He was just pleased that he had been instrumental in helping Alan to discover himself.

Kyle Taylor was an entirely different story. Kyle was Welby-born and bred. He was the same age as Guy and had a youthful, optimistic disposition. Unlike other men on the team, Guy found Kyle to be open and, despite painting his canvas with the same broad, unsubtle strokes as them, a lot more forthcoming and unreserved. Guy enjoyed the time he spent with Kyle immensely and they quickly became close. Kyle even took Guy back to meet his family for a gorgeous home-cooked meal.

Guy felt that something good had clicked between him and Kyle. They were well-matched in humour and general outlook, if obviously not background, and speedily developed an easy, relaxed dimension to their relationship. They often ended up in play-tussles with each other over who had won the last game on the computer or took the mickey out of each other comfortably, knowing the boundaries of where their individual sensitivities lay.

Of course, from Guy's point of view, it helped their friendship a lot that Kyle was so gorgeous. Kyle was very handsome, not pretty, but manly and square-jawed. He had light skin, with a pinkish tinge at the cheeks and his face was often lightly stubbled and framed by a light-brown quiff of hair. He was slightly taller than Guy and his body was in fantastic shape as a result of Welby's intensive training. He had a large frame that wasn't over-muscled like a body builder, but pleasantly shaped, as if it had been developed in the course of hard, manual work like a labourer's. Guy certainly enjoyed taking in the view when he showered next to Kyle after a hard day's exercise or rolled around with him on the floor when they play-fought each other.

Kyle had never made a pass at him and Guy was unsure to what extent his attraction was reciprocated. There were moments when he thought he caught Kyle's looks linger just that little bit too long, but there were no definite signs and, not wanting to spoil their friendship, Guy refrained from acting on his impulses. For the time being, he was happy to appreciate what existed between them. Their friendship, and Alan's, and the positive reception he had received from people like Lambert and Reeves made his initial weeks in Welby a lot easier than they would have been otherwise.

It was in the last few days before the season started that local interest in Guy really began to gather momentum. He found, for the first time since he started playing the game, that he had some significant media interest in him and he ended up doing an interview for *The Welby Gazette*. He met the journalist in a pub in town and found the man to be friendly and yet somewhat wary. He was an older man, who had lived locally all his life and was a long-time fan of the team. Though there was no direct animosity during the meeting, he seemed slightly suspicious of Guy's background and reasons for the switch to League. The journalist showed concern over whether Guy would fit in' and whether he would be accepted, although he held Guy's talents in great admiration. Guy felt he handled the man's doubts and questions well, however, and he left the interview feeling positive. It didn't come as much of a surprise, though, when he actually saw what the man had written about him. The piece wasn't completely negative, but all the journalist's reservations and concerns over the drastic change in the new line-up and Welby's policies for recruiting players in general, were made very clear. Thankfully, the writer did take a wait-and-see attitude, rather than a stance of outright condemnation. Lambert, on the day of publication, rang Guy to reassure him that the journalist was an old stick-in-the-mud and that he had nothing to worry about in terms of Welby welcoming him onboard.

However, Guy couldn't help but wonder whether the article reflected the town's feelings about him as a whole and felt an increase in pressure to prove that the money used to bring him to the team was well spent. More encouragingly, the regional news programme did a feature on him. They filmed him training with the rest of the team and asked him a few questions about how he felt about his move to Welby. He answered enthusiastically, of course, saying how much he had enjoyed his time in the town so far, how greatly he looked forward to his future there and the impending rugby season. A lot of what he said was mere sports-speak and platitudes, but he did manage to put across some of his own individual character, even getting a decent laugh out of the interviewer and film crew when he made a self-deprecating joke about being a 'posh southerner'. He was glad that they included that moment when they broadcast the feature. On the whole, the piece was favourable, concentrating on the pioneering aspects of the transfer, the novelty of a ex-Union player in a League team and the fish-out-of-water slant of the general story. It seemed a very favourable look at Guy, giving a brief overview of what he had achieved in rugby previous to the transfer, and appeared hopeful for the future, especially when Guy compared its tone to the newspaper article. He videotaped the broadcast and sent a copy of it to his mother. The next time he spoke to her on the phone, she almost burst with pride, her concern about his post on the team seemingly all but dissipated.

It was a couple of days after the news programme had aired its piece on him that his first proper game with Welby was to be played. He felt enthusiastic about what was ahead, eager for his first real public outing with the team. That Saturday, he drove to Welby's ground with an extreme case of butterflies in his stomach. He was nervous, partially doubting his ability to perform, but he was also very, very excited. Now he would find out whether it had all been worthwhile and the situation thrilled and scared him in equal measure.

There was a good atmosphere in the changing room before the match. All the men were raring to go, happy that the season had finally started. Kyle was almost giddy at the prospect of playing once more, being very chatty and animated as he changed into his gear. In the main, the other men didn't seem as aloof as they had been, either, as if they had finally got used to the fact that Guy would be playing with them. Only Georgie Grant and a couple of his cronies kept their distance, barely greeting him on his arrival and not really entering into conversation with him.

When the men were more or less fully changed, Lambert interrupted their excited conversations, getting them seated.

"Well, boys," Lambert stood in front of them with his hands held behind his back. "It's the first game of the season again. There've been a lot of changes: most obvious, Roddy Johnson, bit of a key player for us, one helluva fly half, has moved on. But we've got a damn good replacement here with Guy. I'm sure he'll fit in fine and you'll give him great support in his first real game with us."

Guy sensed there was something in the respectful silence that followed Lambert's speech, but whether it was a welcoming air or hint of animosity he couldn't tell. He looked around the men, and then caught Kyle's eye next to him. Breaking the moment, Kyle winked. Guy felt relieved, deciding that there was probably a mixture of both good and bad sentiment towards him.

"We're up against Weston today," Lambert continued. "They're a good team, but they aren't as good as us. They may well give us a run for our money, but we've beaten 'em before. Play well and there should be no trouble and that's all I'm asking from you today. You've trained hard, you're fit and skilled, but there's nothing that can prepare you for playing on the pitch in a proper game like the real thing. You're bound to be a little rusty, but so will they. All you need to do is keep it steady, give us some good, solid playing and the match will be ours. Play like a team, boys. Play like a team."

Guy wondered whether there was any loaded meaning in Lambert's last words. Was it a reference to how he had not fitted in completely to his new team, a warning to those who were keeping him at arm's length? He asked himself whether such guidance would have any effect, but then Jimmy Reeves took Lambert's place and began to reel off a few words of tactical advice and he forced himself to concentrate. Reeves' ideas were straightforward: simple but effective plays, focusing on what he perceived to be Weston's weak spots. He ended by rousing the men, asking them if they were ready to get out and play, and encouraging them to shout back in loud affirmation repeatedly. Guy felt steeled by the booms of the men's voices and, as they finished their dressing, he became increasingly desperate to get out on the pitch and begin the game.

Then the moment arrived. The team left the changing room. Guy became incredibly jittery as he and the other men walked up the tunnel onto the pitch. It was finally hitting home for him as the cheers of the crowd grew from being mere echoes to louder, full-force chants from all sides. His first League game, the first game he had ever been paid money for, his first chance to prove his worth with Welby. It all seemed too much, and yet, at the same time, unbelievably thrilling

Finally, he was there out on the pitch. Playing in front of a crowd was something he had done many times before and yet that day it was different. It had always brought nerves, which diminished as soon as the physical demands and mental concentration came into play, but he could feel them much more in those final moments before the opening whistle blew, increased by the newness of it all and how much he wanted to prove himself. He was so worked up that the match started almost without him noticing, but soon enough he began to calm down as the familiarity of what he was doing took over. Soon he found himself in possession of the ball. He made some headway, causing several Weston players to charge towards him and, almost before he knew it, the ball was out of his hands. Weston thundered past the Welby players and what seemed to Guy to be only seconds later scored the first points of the match. He felt to blame. The moment that had given Weston their chance had sprung from a play he was involved in and, as an initial move in his first game, it didn't bode well for the future.

The rest of the match went by in a similar manner. Every time Welby regained possession, Weston blasted the ball from them, scoring again and again, and the match finished with Weston ahead with one hell of a lead.

Guy was terribly downhearted as he and the rest of the team filed into the changing rooms again, one by one. His first game and it had been a disaster. He truly felt that, though he wasn't entirely to blame for them losing the game, he had failed his new team. There was an air of defeat as the men began undressing. The room was more or less silent, any noise or speech seeming very inappropriate at that point in time. Guy looked around to survey the effects the game had had on the men. They were all devastated by the aftermath, their shoulders slumped, heads down, faces blank, deep in thought or grimacing in outright misery and disappointment. It was all a million miles away from the ebullience and uplift in the room not two hours earlier. Just as Guy had begun to feel that things couldn't get worse, Ron stalked into the changing rooms, angry and disapproving. He told the men to sit down so that he could speak to them once more.

"Bloody shambles out there today. A bloody shambles!" He shook his head, letting his gaze fall unflinchingly on the men one by one. "First game of the season and, if it's any indicator to what's to come, we might as well pack it all in now and give it up as a bad job."

He paused. "Lazy, that's what I'd call it. *Really* lazy playing. Like some school team who've just been introduced to the game. There were moments out there, Georgie," Ron focused his vehemence on Grant, "... when I had no idea what you were doing. Easy tackles that you just missed and for what?"

Grant mumbled something that sounded like a series of swearwords. Ron was more than capable of coping with any backlash.

"You were shite out there, Grant, and you know it!" he shouted. "None of you were much better, mind you! And you know why? Because you weren't together. It was like you were all playing different matches, by yourselves. That's not how you win a game. You lost because you couldn't be a team like I asked."

If Guy had felt bad on entering the changing rooms, he felt even worse now. There was nothing like a dressing-down after a game had gone badly and this particular dressing-down, after this particular game, was hitting home severely. He raised his eyes from the patch of mud on his boot, only to catch the stern stare of Georgie Grant, who was sneering at him from the opposite bench. Lambert was right. The men weren't working as a team and part of what was preventing them from doing so was Guy himself.

"Right," Lambert clapped his hands together, obviously meaning business. "Get changed. I want you upstairs in the players' bar ready to face the public. No drinking, mind, because you'll be training tomorrow."

The men groaned at the thought of relinquishing their day off.

"You start showing me you don't need the practice and I'll stop forcing you into it," Lambert grumbled as he left.

"He's right, you know," Kyle sighed next to Guy as he tugged off a sock. "We were piss-poor today. I don't know what happened. Shame it was your first game and all."

Guy nodded. He felt very despondent.

"Ah well, we can only get better, I suppose."

"You're not wrong there," Guy smiled, glumly. At that moment, he was having trouble sharing his friend's optimism. He pulled off his shorts, and then, finally naked, went to shower.

Guy found the players' bar as subdued as the changing rooms had been, filled with quiet murmuring conversation, rather than lively, upbeat chattering. The fans had obviously been let down by Welby's performance. If the truth be told, he had not wanted to face people in the bar at all. He felt greatly disappointed by what had happened. He had hoped for a much more positive atmosphere in which to first meet Welby fans, with people primed and excited at the chance to talk with the new star player who had contributed so much to a victorious game. The reality, of course, was far different. No one seemed to notice his arrival and he was half-glad for that, wanting merely to keep his profile low until it was time to leave.

It was the first time he had seen the bar filled with people. The place had a wide mixture of clientèle. There were a few families, connected to the players, Guy supposed, groups of men in Welby shirts and colours and older couples who sat at tables on their own. The atmosphere was open, almost familial, and it struck Guy as resembling nothing other than a local pub. He could see how enjoyable an arena it would be to celebrate in after better matches. As it was, it made him feel unsettled and insecure. There were few friendly faces around. Both Lambert and Reeves were already occupied, deep in conversation. Not too far off, he could see Georgie Grant eyeing him. Grant was muttering to a tall, rough-looking man who could easily pass for a bouncer. Guy guessed he would be better off steering clear of the both of them. He was unsure of what to do with himself and was greatly relieved when Kyle entered the bar and walked up to join him.

"Time to drown our sorrows," Kyle shrugged. "In lemonade."

One of the things that Guy liked best about Kyle was his innate stoicism. It appeared he wasn't about to let one discouraging afternoon ruin his appetite for life.

"Cheer up," he nudged Guy with an elbow. "There'll be other matches."

"That's what I'm afraid of!" Guy rolled his eyes.

"Oh, we'll get it together, don't you worry about it." Kyle ordered a couple of drinks.

Guy began to feel marginally better. He guessed the best way to see it was from Kyle's angle: the only way was up from that point. He felt glad to have a friend like Kyle, someone who would cheer him, be optimistic when he just couldn't be. At that moment, he felt a tap on his shoulder. He turned to find a woman standing behind him with an earnest look on her face.

"Excuse me," she began rather nervously. "I wonder if you could sign this for me."

She held out a programme and a pen. "It's for my grandson. He's got all the players' signatures except yours now and he's poorly at the moment. It would cheer him a lot to get it."

The woman had a kind face and she smiled a shaky smile at Guy as he took the pen.

"I'm sorry to hear that. About his illness, I mean." Guy wrote 'Get well soon!' in big letters on the programme. "What's his name?"

"Dean. Oh, it's nothing serious. Well, nothing long-lasting," she corrected herself. "He broke his arm playing rugby with his mates. Meant he couldn't come to see the game."

"He didn't miss much, did he?" Guy joked.

The woman laughed. "Well, I didn't want to pass comment..."

Guy felt relaxed, happy at the attention and the implicit note of acceptance it conveyed to him.

"We'll try harder next time," he said.

"Don't you worry, love. I'm sure you'll settle in fine, given time." She carefully placed the signed programme in her handbag. "And thanks for that!" She tottered off back to her husband. Guy overheard her say something about him being "a lovely young man", quickly followed by the words "well-spoken".

"Things aren't so bad, you see." Kyle passed over a glass of fresh orange. "You've got fans already."

"One down, how many to go?" Guy's spirits had lifted at the brief interaction with the woman. If she and her grandson were seeing him as part of the team, then others were too.

Kyle raised his glass. "Here's to Holbrook's one fan!" he exclaimed, before clinking his drink against Guy's.

Guy felt suddenly conspicuous. He and Kyle were the only ones in the bar who appeared to be enjoying themselves to any degree and were definitely the only players with smiles on their faces. He had just convinced Kyle they ought to put on a semblance of solemnity when he saw the man Georgie Grant had been talking to put down his pint on a nearby table and swagger over to them.

"I bet you anything he doesn't want an autograph," Guy whispered to Kyle, preparing himself for the worst.

"Enjoying yourself, boys?" The man spoke with a thick Welby accent and his expression was one of extreme disdain. He had closely-shaven hair and Guy could see a small tattoo of a bird on his neck just above the collar of his rugby shirt. The man swayed a little as he stood.

"Pleased to meet you," Guy stuck out his hand by way of greeting. "Guy Holbrook. And you are...?"

The man simply shook his head, apparently disgusted by the very idea of shaking hands with Guy.

"You've got some nerve, haven't you?" he growled. "Think you're some kind of big man, better than the rest of us?"

"I'm not entirely sure what you mean," Guy decided he better try and placate the man. "Can I get you a drink and we'll discuss it?"

"I've got my own money, posh boy!" the man shouted.

Guy suddenly felt all the attention in the bar turn on them. Again, he tried to calm the situation.

"Okay, my friend. No offence meant," he attempted a charming smile.

"I'm not your friend, Holbrook." The man's voice was constantly loud now. "I don't know how you dare come round here, at a time like this, shoving where you came from and how great you think you are down our throats. Laughing in the bar after what you done out on the pitch today. It's disgusting!"

The bar was more or less silent. Everyone was listening in to the rantings of the drunken man.

"I'm not sure what you're talking about, but if I've offended you in any way, I'm truly sorry." Guy was doing well at keeping his temper in check in public. He could see the man's fists clenching as he became increasingly worked up.

"Yeah, you've offended me. And there's only one thing you can do about it and that's leave Welby and never come back!"

Realising there was little he could do about the man in such a public place, Guy simply stood and took the insult. Luckily, Kyle was there to intervene.

"Come on, Harris. I think you've had one too many." Kyle moved to stand in between the two men, not seeming intimidated in the slightest. He nodded his head back towards where the man had come from, as if to indicate where he should return.

The man stared at Kyle viciously for a couple of seconds, then turned.

"Don't think you've heard the last of this!" He pointed threateningly at Guy.

"I'm sure I haven't," Guy murmured under his breath to Kyle as the noise in the bar gradually returned to its former level. "Who the hell was that?"

Kyle rolled his eyes and tutted in dismay. "Sorry, Guy. Not the best welcome to Welby, was it? That's Norman Harris."

"He doesn't look much like a Norman." Guy took a sip from his glass, wishing it was something a little stronger

"Most people call him 'Nutter'. And not without reason, either. Talk about an angry young man. He's had more fights than Mike Tyson. You don't want to mess with him, I'm telling you. In his case his bite *is* worse than his bark."

"I gathered *that* much."

"He's always been like that, throwing his weight around. Even at school, he was a bully."

"You go back that far?" Guy asked. "It's hard to believe people like him were ever children."

"Well, he was, for sure. Him and Georgie Grant've been knocking around together ever since the primary. A pretty nasty pair, the both of them. It's just a good job Grant got into rugby to siphon off some of his aggression."

Guy wondered whether Grant had had anything to do with Nutter's outburst. He definitely wouldn't put it past him.

"And what was all that about 'at a time like this'?" Guy suddenly remembered there were parts of what Nutter had said to him that he didn't understand.

"I'll tell you later," Kyle said. "Believe me, it's not the best place to discuss it right now."

Guy dropped the subject. Feeling rather conspicuous as both the new signing and the recent recipient of a public attack on his person, he would have been happy just to leave the bar right there and then. But not wanting to show a loss of face, or for it to seem that Harris had scared him, he stayed until many others had left.

Later on, as he and Kyle were walking through the car park to their respective vehicles, Guy broached the subject of what Harris had said to him.

"I can't believe you've not heard," Kyle said, leaning on the door of his expensive-looking sports car. "It's been in all the papers and the local news. Still, I suppose you've been busy and you're not from round here, either..."

"What is it?" Guy felt confused and a little ashamed of his ignorance.

"Cooper's Mill is closing," Kyle sighed. And then, obviously noticing Guy's bewildered expression, he continued. "It's the hardware factory on the outskirts of town. Big place. Been here for decades. Brought a lot of money into Welby and a lot of jobs. Many families in Welby have got at least one member who's working up at Cooper's. My Mum did for many a year."

The impending damage to the area was obvious to Guy. People out of work, even less cash coming into the area. It was no wonder people were getting upset. And though the feeling was misguided and unfair, he could see how someone who had never known what it was like to go without could get people's backs up at such a sensitive time.

"But why?" Guy asked. "I thought industry exports were one of the things that were actually doing well in Welby."

"They are. But they can do even better with cheaper labour, willing to work longer hours for less pay."

"They're relocating?" The penny had suddenly dropped.

"They've found somewhere in Asia, apparently. It'll make more money for the fat cats long term if they start production over there and close it over here."

"But that's terrible! There must be something that can be done about it."

Kyle shrugged. "Well, the picket line started a few days ago. But I wouldn't hold your breath. You know what these big business types are like. They can do what they want when they want."

The two men stood there in silence for a moment. Guy could feel the shock sinking in. He didn't really know what else to say.

"Anyway, that's one of the things that was troubling Harris." Kyle pressed the button on his key ring, then opened his car door. "He's one of these that will be out of a job in a few months."

Kyle got into his car. He and Guy made their goodbyes. Guy felt despondent as he found his own vehicle and drove home, surprised to find himself feeling sympathy for the man who had started an argument with him in the bar.

Later that evening, Guy rested in front of the television. He felt exhausted, and not only from the physical toll that afternoon's game had taken on his body. It had not been the greatest of days: Welby had lost the match, he had endured an unwarranted torrent of abuse in front of some important Welby fans and, worst of all, he had discovered the reason behind the animosity that he had felt from some quarters since his arrival in the town. He started to feel a little low, not exactly sorry for himself, but definitely up against it. He wondered whether he would ever truly fit into Welby, either the team or the town's community itself. There were some who were behind him, of course. Lambert was still in his corner and he had rung Guy earlier to congratulate him on his conduct in front of Harris in the bar. And if there was one woman and her grandson who were interested in his arrival, there would be others, but he couldn't help feeling that, having been part of that afternoon's failure on the pitch, he had let the people of Welby down. At a time when they had been hit by so much disappointment, a team so popular, so important to the town needed to give its fans hope, a break from their daily worries, and the encouragement to feel that desires can be fulfilled with determination and fighting spirit. That afternoon had given them anything but. He was also, as Nutter Harris had so eloquently pointed out, a man who was very different from the average Welbian. His well-off background would hardly be the first aspect of his character that would make people warm to him at the moment. He began to feel alienated as he grew increasingly tired, lying there on the sofa, his eyes drooping as he half-watched a documentary.

Never one to give up easily, however, his sleepy mind began filtering over plans to make things better. Surely there were ways by which he could change the lie of the land, not only in terms of feeling towards himself, but also of the prospects for the inhabitants of Welby. First, he decided that his team must never lose another game, at least not so badly and shamefully as they had done that day. That could be done in two ways: on an individual level, he could train harder and make himself as good a player as he ever would be (and that, he decided he could start the very next day), and, as a team, they would have to pull together and work as a cohesive unit. That would mean overcoming any differences they had between them, the most obvious being how he and Georgie Grant were pulling in different directions. This, he knew, would be a lot more difficult to attain than to increase his personal fitness and skill. It would rely on other people, for a start. He had no clear ideas at that point how he would do such a thing, but he was determined to do so, and left that part of the planning to another day.

He also decided to show the people of Welby how much he wanted to fit in, how much he was behind them in their hour of need. One way he could do that sprang immediately to mind. He had never been on strike before, having never come across the need to make protests about employment, and he wasn't entirely sure what would be required of him, but he made a promise to himself that the first chance he got he'd be down at the picket line outside Cooper's Mill. If nothing else, it would bring some media attention to a worthy cause.

Five

The next day Guy put his plans into action. He made a real effort with training and, as he had promised himself, stayed after his session with Reeves to put in some more work at the gym, which he promised himself to repeat every other day.

It was on the Tuesday, after noticing Guy's increased efforts earlier in the week, that Kyle Taylor decided to join him after training. Guy was glad of the company. Exercise always seemed to go easier when he was with someone else. It was definitely less lonely for a start and it was always good to have someone to train against and use as a benchmark for what he could achieve. Their relationship being what it was, it wasn't long before the two of them had gone past training against each other and moved on to head-to-head but amiable competition.

"Come on," Kyle encouraged, as Guy strained himself against the bar of the bench press. "You can do better than that!"

Guy pushed the weight up a few more times until he had reached the week's required level of reps, then, panting, sat up.

"All right," he said, wiping the sweat from his brow. "Let's see you have a go."

Kyle took his place and began. He put in as much effort as Guy had and Guy guessed that the two of them were pretty evenly matched.

"I bet I can beat you on the leg raises!" Kyle leapt up from the bench press and moved onto the next machine.

The contest continued throughout their time in the gym.

Eventually, Guy had to acquiesce to Kyle's superior strength, the result of his longer time as a professional rugby player, but Guy was encouraged by the fact that he didn't seem too far behind.

Exhausted but happy, they entered the changing rooms to clean themselves up and get changed. As Guy undressed, he became aware that Kyle was watching him.

"Bloody hell!" Kyle exclaimed. "We must've been working hard. You're pretty pumped up."

Guy looked down at his body. It did seem pretty buff from the exercise.

"Not as much as mine, of course," Kyle joked. "Here, let's compare biceps."

He flexed his arm in the stereotypical body-builder pose.

"All right, then," Guy agreed. The competitive spirit was continuing. He took his shirt off, then tensed his arm and moved it close to Kyle's.

"Not much in it, really," Kyle shrugged, lifting up the leg of his shorts. "How about quads?"

Again, Guy moved closer to Kyle so they could examine each other's bodies more closely.

"Know what, Guy?" Kyle said, "I think you beat me. Your legs are slightly bigger."

Kyle took off his trainers and socks. "But I guess there's only one muscle on a man's body where size really counts."

"Oh yeah, and where's that?" Guy grinned in anticipation.

Kyle whipped off his shorts and threw them into his bag. "Down here, mate," he said pointing to his crotch.

Guy looked at Kyle's wry, cheeky grin, then downwards to where Kyle's fingers were directing his attention. Although he'd seen Kyle undressed many times in the shower and in the changing rooms, it was the first time he had had a proper chance to really examine his friend's genitals. Closer inspection proved rewarding: Kyle's piece, though flaccid, was meaty and sizeable.

It hung about four inches long in front of two large balls that just begged to be handled. It was circumcised, its head looked slightly squashed in shape and was a gorgeous light-pink colour. There was a good garden of pubic hair growing out of Kyle's lower belly, surrounding the base of his dick and spread around his testicles and between his legs. The hair was dark, much darker than that on his head, and as a masculine decoration of one of Guy's favourite places on a man's body, it made his mouth water.

"Not bad. You show-off!" Guy laughed, tugging at a shoelace. He was incredibly aroused at Kyle's shameless abandon, his complete ease and lack of embarrassment at displaying his naked body.

"I'm serious!" Kyle leant over and twanged the elastic of Guy's shorts with a finger. "The competition's not over yet. Come on, let's see who wins on this one."

Guy hesitated. Was pulling his leg or did he really want to see his piece? A couple of seconds passed and Kyle didn't move or change his expectant expression, so Guy thought he might as well play along.

"Okay, then." Guy remained seated and pulled down his shorts. "Have a good look at this."

Though Kyle's man-meat was far from small, Guy was proud of this own cock, so happily exposed himself.

He had been hot in his shorts and, suddenly freed, he felt the pleasant sensation of his sweat gently cooling in the air. He liked the pressure of the bench against his naked arse, the touch of his seat against his dangling balls and, most of all, the attention Kyle was paying to his crotch. He loved having another man look at him like that and it was all he could to do concentrate on other things, to hold back the rush of blood aching to surge and fill his manhood in appreciation.

Kyle put his head on one side as he eyed Guy's genitals. "Stand up," he said.

Guy did as he was told, removing his shorts at the same time. Kyle positioned him, as if trying to get Guy into a better light.

"Pretty evenly matched, I'd say," There was still humour in his demeanor that suggested the situation was nothing but a silly game to him. Guy tried to match the mood with smiles and brief, laddish comments, but he wondered just how well he was managing to hide his state of arousal

"There's only one way to really tell," Kyle nonchalantly scratched between his legs, making his penis dance delightfully.

"And what's that?" Guy could only hope at what was on his team-mate's mind.

"We'll have to check 'em out when they're... you know," Kyle gave a sharp nod. "When they're full, we'll see," he beamed, looking extremely self-satisfied.

"You want us to get erections?" Guy said, as if shocked. He pretended to think about it for a moment and then acquiesced. "Well, I'm game if you are."

"Somehow, I knew you would be," Kyle laughed, nudging Guy with an elbow. His hands went straight to his crotch. He pulled on the end of his prick a few times and squeezed his balls with his other hand. "Come on, then. I want to see what you're made of."

Feeling that it was all still a game to Kyle and entirely safe for him to follow suit, Guy began to masturbate. Already aroused by the sight of Kyle and the horny situation he had created, the stimulation felt great. At last he was able to let go, let himself become hard, to feel the pleasure of sexual touches he had desired so much since the game in the changing rooms had begun. He was very, very excited and felt breathless as if he had exercised. This 'play' put a calmer and more relaxing strain on his body, undercut as it was by primal and fantastic joys. He could hardly believe his luck: here he was, jerking off with his buddy, a man he found greatly attractive and for whom he had been harbouring a secret longing since more or less their first meeting.

The sight of Kyle in an excited state was far from disappointing. He was standing with his legs splayed slightly so that his large thighs extended and grew while he tossed himself off with abandon. His face was wincing slightly with delight and from time to time, he smiled at Guy, obviously completely comfortable with what they were doing together. He kept looking down at what Guy was doing to his own genitals and this added aspect of voyeurism and exhibitionism made Guy feel hot.

Before long, both of them were fully erect.

"Let's have a look, then," Kyle said. He moved over to stand next to Guy and the sides of their thighs and buttocks rubbed against each other briefly. Guy let go of himself. His dick bounced a couple of times and then he saw it throb as an uncontrolled rush of blood surged into it.

Kyle stood so that his and Guy's stiff members were parallel. Guy took another good look at him. Erect, Kyle's penis was chunky and covered in a pattern of tiny veins. Filled, the head that had seemed squashed now looked tastily round and its pink colour had deepened almost to scarlet. It was slightly less wide than the length that supported it, but to Guy it looked the perfect adornment to a particularly attractive piece. Kyle held it by the base. He wobbled it, then rubbed the end as if to keep himself pleasured and, in turn, his penis engorged. He stared down directly at Guy's own prick, then looked back at his own, obviously summing up what was on offer.

"Still not much in it," he said, sounding a little breathless. "You've got me on length a bit and I beat you in girth."

Having perused both dicks very carefully, Guy had to agree.

"I say we call it a draw," Kyle said, moving away.

Guy felt disappointed. Was that it? Had the game been just that, nothing but a bit of mucking around, to end there with him horny and unsatisfied? Fortunately, it seemed Kyle had other ideas in mind.

"Shame, that," he smirked, wryly. "I was sure I'd have you beat."

"You're a cocky bastard sometimes, Kyle," Guy joked, somewhat despondently taking a towel from his bag.

"Hey, pack it in or I'll call in my forfeit on you." Kyle clicked his fingers, as if an idea had suddenly popped into his mind. "That's a thought. You owe me a favour, don't you?"

"Ye-es," Guy said, unsure.

"I think this is a good time to get it repaid. Look at me," Kyle pointed to his crotch again. "I'm as horny as fuck. And this thing isn't going anywhere until I do something about it."

"And how does that involve me, exactly?" Guy played dumb. He knew what Kyle wanted, but wanted to hear him say it.

"Come on, Guy, I know what you're like. You're into all this stuff, aren't you? I'm sure you can help me out somehow."

Guy stood directly in front of Kyle and looked deep into his eyes. A centimetre closer and their cocks would have touched each other's bodies and they would have been able to feel their breath on each other's faces.

"What'll it be?" Guy asked, incredibly eager to meet whatever request Kyle had for him.

"How's about a bit of a suck? That's just the kind of thing I need right now."

"No problem." Guy fell to his knees. "If that's what you want, that's what you can have."

He looked up at Kyle, who was watching him intently. The view was fantastic: a large, handsome man with a dreamy, desirous expression on his face and hands on his hips. Kyle's eager erection quivered a little in front of Guy, who took hold of it at the bottom to steady it, then slowly moved forward. He stuck out his tongue and licked the underside, causing Kyle to moan a grateful "Oh mate!" Guy waggled his tongue around Kyle's bell end a little before taking it into his mouth fully. Kyle was very hard and his round glans felt like a gobstopper against Guy's cheeks as he took it further back. Gradually, Guy took in more and more of his friend, loving every inch of the thick man-meat as it eased inside him. He moved his head back and forth a few times, all the while sucking and letting the saliva coat the piece to lubricate it well. Kyle was loving it, and placed his hands upon Guy's shoulders in a delicate and affectionate manner. Guy put his arms around him, placing his hands on Kyle's firm, taut buttocks, then drew in the man towards him. Relaxing his throat, Guy took the penis in fully so that his nose and lips were buried in Kyle's bush of pubes. They tickled the front of his face gently, as the firm length penetrated his oral cavity forcefully. He swallowed repeatedly and squirmed his tongue to pleasure the thing even more and the moans and puffs of breath Kyle made indicated his work was being greatly enjoyed. He felt fantastic, being crammed with his buddy's jolt like that and, as he began to make regular moves up and down it, he took hold of his own steely manhood and started to play with it.

He found himself rock-hard and more than ready for stimulation. He continued sliding up and down Kyle for a while and then let him spring free from his lips. He moved his head downwards, nuzzling his chin between Kyle's thighs so he could gain access to his balls. The area was still heated from exercise and he could feel the dampness of Kyle's sweat upon his cheeks as he rubbed the gap with his face. The smell was exquisite, a musk only to be found on that particular part of a man's body, and was exceptionally pungent right then. Guy took in a few deep breaths and his body shivered. Unable to hold off any longer, he ran his tongue up the crack of Kyle's thighs, where his cock and balls met his body. The taste was fantastic, salty and meaty, and he loved the sensation of hairs and skin upon his tongue. He licked again and again, then moving right between Kyle's legs, he took one of his testicles into his mouth and caressed it gently. It had the same testosterone-filled flavour and odour as he had found at the side, only much stronger, more exciting. Guy took hold of Kyle's piece as he munched away at his buddy's ball sac, wanking it steadily as he did the same to himself.

"Bloody hell, that's good!" said Kyle. "I guess you know your way around, don't you, having one yourself."

"It's not like when girls do it, is it?" Guy rested his cheek upon Kyle's warm, hairy leg, before he dived back in for more.

"No," Kyle agreed. "It's not like when girls do it."

Before long, Guy could feel a warm, sticky fluid coating the ring his fingers made. Kyle's dick was lubricating itself for the next stage. The thing made little, wet clacking noises as he pulled on it and his thumb and forefinger felt pleasantly tacky. He checked it out, bending the member down a little so that the end faced him directly. The slit at the end glistened with a drop of pre-come. Looking up, he saw Kyle was still watching him intently. He stuck his tongue out and with the very tip licked at the clear blob of juice. He swallowed, savouring the taste greedily, then took the head in his mouth again. He sucked at it a few more times, Kyle's groans much deeper than previously, before Kyle placed his hand on Guy's jawline to stop him.

"Oh, mate. I could have that all night," he said, as he pulled himself away, causing Guy's lips to smack together. "But don't you think it's time you got in on the action?"

Guy shrugged, feigning nonchalance. "It's my forfeit," he reminded Kyle.

"I think you've paid me back more than enough. And besides, as I always say, 'One good turn deserves another'."

He pulled Guy up. Guy was amazed how comfortable Kyle seemed with it all as their cocks bounced next to and over each other.

Kyle smiled. He took hold of Guy's cock, gave it a hearty squeeze, then gave his balls a good fondle with his other hand.

"Well, here goes nothing!" he said, bending over.

Guy felt the wet, comfortable warmth of Kyle's mouth upon

him. At first, he could sense it just on the end, and then quickly the pleasure engulfed him almost to the base. Kyle mouth-shafted him a couple of times, then lowered himself to a squatting position. Though it was obvious from his lack of finesse that it was the first blowjob Kyle had ever given, Guy thought he was pretty good for a beginner. What he lacked in technique, he made up for in enthusiasm. He took Guy far back inside his mouth without much hassle at all and even seemed to be enjoying it, jerking himself off with a heavy-handed, pounding rhythm. The sight of his handsome mouth on Guy's prick was something else, the length disappearing inside him again and again. Guy couldn't take his eyes off him. He wanted that vision to burn in his memory bank of great sexual encounters forever.

Eventually, Kyle backed off, but still held Guy's dick in his hand, as if he didn't want it to disappear or go too far from his grasp.

"How was that?" he asked, his lips shiny from drool and man-juice.

"Not bad at all," Guy panted.

"First time I've done anything like that," Kyle said, not boasting, or being sheepish, merely stating a fact.

"Did you like it?" Guy shivered as Kyle casually pulled on his length.

"Damn right, I did," Kyle said. He stood up. "And I'll tell you something else. I want to try some more."

He took Guy by the waist with both hands. The movement was gentle, affectionate, much more like a lover might make rather than a friend. Again, their stiff cocks bounced into each other, their ends rubbing over the skin of each other's legs.

"You've got me horny as hell, Kyle," Guy confessed. "I'd be up for just about anything right now. What's your poison?"

"Well, I heard you guys are either givers or takers, aren't you?"

Guy laughed inwardly at the man's lack of awareness, despite his recent first-hand practical knowledge. "Some of us aren't so choosy. Which would you prefer me to be?"

Kyle pulled Guy in closer. Their dicks lay on their lower bellies and began to squirm against each other.

"Right now, Guy, I'd really like to know what it feels like to be inside another man. Right now, I really want to put it up you."

Kyle looked longingly into Guy's eyes as he spoke. Guy wondered whether to risk a kiss and decided that if Kyle wanted to he would.

"I thought you'd never ask," he smiled. "Come on, then big boy. Show me what you've got."

He gave Kyle's buttocks a hefty whack with the palm of his hand, then quickly jumped away out of his friend's reach.

"You cheeky fucker!" Kyle leapt after him, his arms outstretched.

"You can have it if you can catch me!" Guy exclaimed, knowing he wasn't about to try too hard to escape.

The two men began a game of tag. Kyle stood in front of Guy, his legs splayed and his arms wide ready to tackle him. His dick waggled enticingly as he moved. Guy matched his position, and then, as if he was on the pitch, feinted and set off the opposite way. It was an intentionally poor dummy, however, and Kyle grabbed him in a big hug around the waist and tackled him to the ground.

The tiles of the floor were cold and hard against Guy's body, but having a decently sized naked man taking him in a strong hold was quite some compensation. He half-heartedly tried to fight Kyle off but, being on top, his friend had the advantage. They mock-wrestled, as they had so many times before, but it had never been so erotic for Guy. Kyle's meaty arms and chest pressed against him. He could feel his buddy's still-erect penis pushing and rubbing against his leg and his own cock teased by the skin and weight of the body upon him. Gradually, Kyle eased himself up Guy's body, pinning him to the ground completely.

"You win!" Guy panted.

"You weren't even trying," Kyle looked deep into Guy's eyes once more. "You really want it, don't you?"

Guy winked. Kyle's body relaxed a little and he moved his head downwards.

"Well, I'll just have to give it to you then, won't I?" His face was centimetres from Guy's. "Exactly how you want it."

And then he kissed Guy. It was as tentative an action as his attempt at a blowjob. And yet it was no less pleasurable. He had firm lips that planted themselves solidly upon Guy's, before they began to move, slowly and unsurely at first, then with gradual confidence more and more eagerly. Guy responded in kind, not forcing himself on Kyle too rapidly, just following his friend's lead and doing what he did until the inevitable happened. Kyle's tongue began probing his mouth, in shy experimental steps at first and then became increasingly daring and ferocious. Soon, the two men were at each other's mouths like animals at the trough, fencing with their lips and tongues as if their lives depended on it. Their bodies locked, their arms gripped each other tightly and they began to rub against each other, taking great pinches of each other's flesh into their hands as they lost themselves in ecstasy.

Guy took hold of one of Kyle's hands and moved it up to where their faces met. He directed Kyle's middle finger into the space where their tongues fought against each other, then took it into his mouth to get it good and wet. He guided the hand back downwards once more and then opening his legs wider, pointed the finger along the crack of his arse. Kyle braced himself a little and then Guy felt the finger trace the rim of his anus all of its own accord. The delicate touches made his bumhole tingle with joy as his sensitive nerve endings were stimulated.

"Stick it up there, Kyle," he whispered into his friend's ear. "It'll make it easier for me before we go any further."

They stopped kissing as Guy felt the digit make its first move inwards. He let himself relax and breathed deeper, trying to let the muscles of his rectum open up more around his chum.

"Go on," he encouraged. "It'll get easier in a bit."

The finger forced its way upwards and almost immediately Guy felt himself ease a little. Then he made a conscious effort to squeeze Kyle.

"Imagine that, Kyle," he said. "Imagine that tightness around your prick."

Kyle removed his finger slowly, then taking one of Guy's legs in each hand, lifted them up.

"Let me have a look at it," he said. "I like to see what I'm letting myself in for."

Guy felt Kyle poking around a little, lifting his balls and spreading his cheeks so that he could have a good look up his crack. It was delightfully erotic: not only that he was exposing himself like that, but because he guessed that it was the first time Kyle had really examined another man's body in such a close and sexual manner. He felt fingers tickling his hole, probing it, and then one was fully inserted once more. It pushed up him and then back out and then repeated the motion a few times before it was fully withdrawn.

Kyle spat onto his fingers. Guy noticed for the first time what large hands he had. Two of his digits went a good way to providing the width of his dick, if not the length, and Guy thrilled at the thought of having them inside him.

"Ready for more?" Kyle asked, a string of spittle dangling from his middle finger.

"Am I ever," Guy murmured. He felt the sensation of something larger poking at him. His arse fought against it at first, but gently, it forced its way in and began to waggle around. Guy moaned at the pain of the insertion. It hurt, for sure. But what a pain! What a glorious, fantastic pain!

And then, without much grace, but with a definite pleasure-inducing effect, Kyle began to finger-fuck him in a hard, almost clumsy way. Short, jerky stabs at first, then movement became easier, long, slow prodding at him that made him groan at every insertion.

"In my bag, Kyle," Guy sighed eventually, loving it but wanting more. "The side pocket. You'll find condoms. And those other small packets are lube."

Kyle moved over to the bench by their side. "They're what?" he asked as he delved in the bag.

"Lubricant," Guy explained, loving every minute of Kyle's ignorance. "It'll just make things a little easier for us both."

Despite his subordinate state earlier on, having had to pay back his favour to Kyle, Guy had begun to feel aroused: he was introducing Kyle to the enjoyment men can have together, initiating his friend, teaching him what was what in the realm of gay sex. What made it even better was having such a willing, eager and attractive pupil.

"I see," Kyle nodded. He opened the condom packet carefully and then rolled one on himself. He was ready to learn, not embarrassed or self-conscious about his limited knowledge. Guy had often seen him this way when Reeves had gone through some team tactics.

"Come on then, mate. Sort it out." Kyle obviously needed a little more guidance. His dick, now sheathed, looked as attractive as ever in its shiny, greasy new coat of wrinkled rubber. Indicating the height of Kyle's arousal, it remained hard as he ripped open the square of lube. Some of it squirted out onto his fingers immediately.

"Whoops!" he said, surprised, as it dripped over his hands.

Guy smiled, once more taken by his friend's naivety in the situation. "Put some on me," he directed. "And get some on yourself."

Kyle knelt down. Guy flinched as his friend wiped some of the cold liquid over his tender ringpiece. It felt cool and soothing after the relative warmth and roughness of Kyle's saliva-coated fingers earlier and he shivered as a couple of digits slipped inside him, much more smoothly than they had before.

"Bloody works, this stuff, doesn't it?" Kyle said, pleased, as he squirted out the rest of the packet onto himself. He rubbed his dick up and down a couple of times to coat it fully, then paused and looked a little bemused.

"What's up?" Guy asked. Kyle seemed momentarily embarrassed.

"Well, I've never even had a woman up there before. I'm just wondering how you guys do it."

Guy smiled. "It's straightforward enough." He raised his legs so that his quads lay upon his belly and chest again. His arse raised expectantly. "Get on top of me," he encouraged his friend. "I'll guide you in."

Kyle did as he was told. He hooked himself under Guy's calves and outstretched his arms, placing a hand either side of Kyle's shoulders. His warm, hard body felt fantastic on the underside of Guy's thighs and Guy could feel his buddy's hard, hot tumescence poking around at his entrance. He reached for it and directed it to his hole with his fingers.

"Now push in," he told his friend. "Slowly, though."

Once more, Kyle obeyed. Guy closed his eyes, concentrating on relaxing his rectal muscles as the thick member gradually pushed its way inside him. The pain returned, but he bore it, knowing all the while what was in store for him.

"You all right?" Kyle asked, obviously worried about the damage he might be causing his chum.

Already the pain was subsiding, giving way to the unparalleled ecstasy of being filled with man-meat. Guy opened his eyes again. "Yeah," he half-moaned. "That's just how it's supposed to be."

"Thank God for that," Kyle said, relieved. "Because I really didn't want to take it out again. It's so tight, Guy. It's bloody gorgeous!"

Guy looked up at Kyle's handsome, reddening face. "Now fuck me," he demanded. "Take it steady at first, while I loosen up some more. Soon enough you'll be doing it like you would to a woman."

"You don't need to tell me twice," Kyle murmured as he pulled back gently. Cautiously he pushed back, obviously enjoying the sensation greatly and then repeated the motion. With every movement, Guy felt his arse muscles relaxing more and, while the pain remained at a certain level, it became enjoyable rather than uncomfortable, a wonderful experience for his delicate nerve endings, stimulating and erotic. He put his hands on Kyle's hard buttocks to control him, guiding the speed and force of each thrust, until he reached a point where he could let his friend make his own pace.

"Go on, a bit faster now," he encouraged. Gradually, Kyle increased the pace of each inward push. Guy let go of him and ran his hands over the man's firm, wide back, over his exercise-increased shoulders and neck. Guy raised his head up a little and pulled Kyle down to him. They kissed again. This time there was no apprehensiveness: both men went in straight for the kill, their mouths fighting against each other in horny abandonment. Without further direction, Kyle began pumping harder, so that his body began regularly slamming into Guy's. The room echoed with the soft slaps of skin upon skin, of the grunts of both men as they lost themselves in pleasure and each other. Kyle was all over Guy now and Guy loved it. He had a real man in his arms, at his lips. Kyle felt heavy on him and yet it was a fantastic burden to bear and he was a willing receptacle for Kyle's joy. Kyle was becoming more animalistic as he shunted up him again and again, but at the same time was becoming connected to him, wanting and needing Guy to bring to him to even higher peaks. Kyle raised himself up again, holding his body up so that his thrusts became direct and accurate. Seizing the chance, Guy slipped a hand over his belly, taking hold of his own erection. It was very sticky now. There was a mess around his navel where his dick had pressed against him and he wiped some of it over himself before he began to wank. He didn't need soft touches now. Now was the time for some rough handling. He was fucking hot, not far from his own climax, but wanting to wait until Kyle was ready. He teased himself with his finger, but stopped before he got carried away. Before long, Kyle's body began to tense. His fucks were machine-like, forceful and regular. Guy knew what to do to bring his friend over the edge. Though his rectum fought against it, he squeezed the muscles of his entrance tighter, feeling Kyle's hard dick become even more enclosed by him as Kyle thundered away. The trick worked straightaway. Kyle gazed deep into Guy's eyes with an almost worried expression and then, with one almighty shunt forward, his face grimaced with ecstasy. Guy felt all Kyle's muscles harden then relax as the man's almighty prick triggered again and again up his chute. A drip of sweat fell from Kyle's brow onto Guy as Kyle's contorted expression altered into one of dreamy joy as his orgasm lessened. He leant back, obviously exhausted but happy.

"Now me," Guy asked, ready for his turn. Kyle took hold of his dick and started to stroke him, taking a handful of his balls at the same time. Guy looked at his friend, the tingling sensations at his prick increasing by the second. Kyle was so good-looking, his body so attractive and on top of that, he was such a nice guy. Guy began to feel something that wasn't love in a romantic sense, but as deep on another level. It was sexual attraction, definitely, but also close, close friendship, as close as he had felt with anyone ever. And what they were doing right there and then was a perfect expression of what he felt for Kyle. It could only serve to bring them closer.

Guy was at his peak now. His body shivered and he closed his eyes, almost unable to take the joy he felt inside. The tension within him grew as Kyle yanked away at his cock, the build-up of pressure intense as his entire being prepared itself for what was to come. He heard a moan, then realised he'd made it, lost as he was in physical nirvana. And then everything exploded within him. Wave after wave of fantastic thrills washed over him. His dick pumped away uncontrollably in Kyle's hands, the first shot being so strong that it streaked up his torso, hitting him on the chin. Again and again, he was coated with heated creamy fluid and he raised his head to watch the drips cover his skin and the hands of his friend. It was a glorious, beautiful sight.

As his climax subsided, he licked at the blob of his own jizz that had landed by his mouth.

"Waste not, want not," he winked at Kyle. Kyle laughed. Then, easing himself out of Guy, he let his friend's legs down so that they could lie together more comfortably. Side by side, they cuddled and kissed each other tenderly, the mess made by Guy's come cooling and dribbling over the skin where their bellies touched.

"Not bad for a first-timer," Guy smiled at his friend in between pecks.

"Thanks," Kyle grinned. "I'm looking forward to the second time!"

Guy felt great lying there in his buddy's arms. Warm with afterglow, the situation seemed good and right. He sensed a shift in his and Kyle's relationship, as if the sex had brought them closer together, as if a special bond had grown between them that would have never existed if they hadn't begun their silly challenge game earlier on that day. He wondered if Kyle felt it too, but at that moment, it seemed too amorphous to put into words. Not wanting to break the easy, relaxed moment, he left it and simply enjoyed the straightforward pleasure of being naked with, and physically close to, a good friend.

It was with great disappointment that Guy entered the showers with Kyle. He could have easily spent much more time with his friend, but knew their showering only brought the moment of parting closer. And part they did, going their separate ways that evening much later than expected.

Guy returned home tired, but satisfied. The spring in his step that had been missing since his arrival in Welby had returned and he felt happy and once more eager to face the challenge that the move presented him with. His afterglow burned long and bright within him, changing his outlook for the better. For a good few hours, he couldn't stop thinking about what had happened and how glad he was of the shift in their relationship it possibly signified. He checked himself mentally, realising it wasn't love he felt or mere lust, but something else entirely, something that he couldn't quite put his finger on and yet that seemed great and utterly perfect for where they both were in their lives. He went to bed that night care-free, feeling entirely refreshed and positive for the future and had the best night's sleep he had had in a long time.

Six

In the morning, Guy found his feelings of positivity had diminished but not fully disappeared and they remained as a backdrop to his general thoughts as he performed his daily tasks. He went to that day's training with the same eagerness he had felt on his first day at Welby. His only worry as he walked into the changing rooms was whether Kyle would be shy with him, or stand-offish, having decided the night before was a mistake. But to Guy's delight, Kyle was as relaxed and buoyant as he had been when he had left him. As they changed next to each other, in the very same place where they had made love not twenty-four hours before, Kyle showed no signs at all of any concern or bad feeling towards him. Instead, he seemed energetic and enthusiastic at being in his presence, telling jokes and ribbing him and was as physical as he had ever been. Guy laughed inwardly at his behaviour. Kyle was like a playful young puppy and Guy lapped it up, delighted.

During training, Guy found that the exercises the team performed seemed a lot tighter than before. Reeves made him and Kyle do a lot of close work together, which he enjoyed greatly. Whether it was all in his mind, or whether the changes had actually occurred he couldn't tell, but their playing did seem to have improved. It was as if they were becoming used to each other's moves. It felt as if a link between them was growing so that they could guess and predict what each other would do next. They were building a closeness and familiarity that meant their playing was a lot smoother and less haphazard.

With the other men on the team, basic standards also seemed to have gone up a notch. There were fewer dropped passes, fewer dodged tackles and morale and team spirit seemed to have gone up since the disappointments of their last match. One problem still remained for Guy and that was the animosity from Grant. He made it clear that he was still unable to accept Guy as either a friend or a team-mate. When he wasn't simply ignoring Guy, he was trying to provoke him or put him down. Guy couldn't understand it. He thought Grant would at least attempt to get on with him for the sake of the team. But the barrier that had built up between them seemed impenetrable and the best Guy could hope for between them was a basic standard of playing.

In general, however, Guy felt a lot more positive when the following weekend's match came around. Lambert's pre-match talk was stern, "not wanting a repeat of the previous week's game", but also encouraging. Lambert had put time in training with the men and seen how they had begun to gel as a team. It was that kind of playing that he wanted see out there that day, he told the team, and for the first time Guy felt that they truly could do exactly what their manager wanted.

As they went out onto the pitch, Guy sensed a strange atmosphere. The fans were noisy, obviously happy to see their team, and yet they were holding back a little, as if the blow of the defeat last week, in addition to the broadly felt sense of despair boded ill for the season and they were unsure of what Welby would show them that afternoon. The team they faced, Lambert had pointed out, was one that should pose them a challenge but, under the right conditions, was well within their capabilities to defeat.

The early part of the game went well. Reflecting what happened in that week's training, Welby's performance was tighter than it had been before and soon they were racking up some respectable points on the board. Although the team as a whole seemed to have improved, it was Guy and Kyle who provided a key force in their general strategy. The two men worked closely together and brought on the plays that pushed their team forward again and again. After a while, Guy could sense a change in the mood of the spectators. Excitement returned and there was an almost tangible air of anticipation whenever he or Kyle got hold of the ball.

There were still some mistakes. During the later part of the game, Welby's earlier focus began to shake a little and the opposing team pushed their score upwards. The old trouble with Grant hadn't gone away and there were moments when the lack of trust between them inhibited the teams progress, losing them possession. It was not the greatest match ever played. But it was still one hell of a lot better than what they had managed to achieve before and Welby won, albeit narrowly. The cheers of the crowd as the final whistle blew made up for the disappointment of the week before. They were elated and if not fully overjoyed at what had happened that afternoon, at least sounded encouraged and hopeful.

Back in the locker room, Lambert was full of praise.

"Well done, boys!" he beamed, as the men, exhausted, sweaty and dirty, filed past him to peel off their kit. "That's the kind of stuff I want to see. Teamwork. That's the only thing that'll work. There were plenty of moments there when you were as cohesive and purposeful as you should be. Got shaky towards the end, didn't it? But at least you stopped 'em from taking over fully. I'm glad to see the improvement and I bet you are, too."

"Does this mean we get a bonus?" shouted Gripper Mason, obviously only half joking.

"No, it bloody does not! And don't think I'm going to be taking it easier on you from now on. We've still got a long way to go, especially if we want to be in with a chance for the Cup. Training's going to be as hard as it was last week..."

A general groan echoed around the room.

"… but as a treat you can have tomorrow off for a change." Lambert made to leave as the groan changed to a mock expression of thankfulness.

"Hey, don't be saucy." Lambert stopped himself from leaving. "Just one more thing, guys. I'd like to make a special mention of Holbrook and Taylor. There was some bloody encouraging play out there from those two, some great displays of togetherness and team-play thinking."

Lambert turned to address Guy and Kyle directly. "Now I know you two – especially you, Guy – have been putting in some extra work. Well, it's obviously paying off. Keep it up. Whatever you've done, some of the others could do with as well. Maybe you could give them a few pointers."

Guy felt embarrassed but happy that his efforts had been noticed. He looked at Kyle, who gave him a pleased but not cocky smile and a shrug as he pulled off his shirt to reveal his gorgeous body.

Kyle's naked torso was a sight Guy never tired of, not even now they had had sex. He could smell Kyle's sweat in the air. It was fresh, the kind produced by hard labour, contact sports or lovemaking. And with that thought it suddenly struck Guy: it was the lovemaking between Kyle and himself that had brought them together, that had been the catalyst that had finally improved their skills together on the pitch. It couldn't have been anything else. The sudden confirmation in his mind made his spirits soar. Guy's train of thought was suddenly interrupted by Lambert.

"As for you, Grant," Lambert sounded stern. "A word, please."

Lambert took Grant to one side. Their conversation was obviously not meant to be overheard by the rest of the team, but not to go unnoticed by them, either. As Guy changed, he couldn't help earwigging some of what was going on and notice the expressions on the two men's faces. Neither looked particularly happy and both frequently grimaced in anger. Guy heard Lambert mentioning teamwork a lot, talking about how rugby is not a game played by one man alone, and then shuddered as Grant audibly spat out the name 'Holbrook'. Lambert lowered his voice even further after that and Guy, not sure he even wanted to hear any more, concentrated on undressing himself.

Grant and Lambert were still arguing when Guy went to get clean. When he returned, Grant was on the bench removing his boots and socks. Guy caught Grant's eye and met a mean, unfriendly stare. Guy nodded by way of brief greeting, deciding not to bother the man too much right then. He felt good about how the match had gone and was still happy about his realisation concerning the improvement in his and Kyle's playing. He decided not to let Grant get to him. He knew things would have to change eventually. Grant would have to listen to Lambert in the long run, if not for the team's sake, for his own.

Seven

The next day was a good one for Guy. He woke later than usual, feeling he really deserved his day off, and decided to do with it just exactly what he pleased. And that meant very little. He spent the morning making a big fry-up, which wasn't exactly on his list of approved foods in terms of training, but seemed appropriate and justified anyway. He then read the entirety of the Sunday paper while drinking a big pot of coffee. He made a few phone calls to friends and his parents, then relaxed on the sofa in the afternoon, watching a stupid but entirely enjoyable action movie on pay-per-view on his widescreen television. After that, he sorted out the contents of a couple of boxes that still needed emptying from the move, placing things in the right cupboards or on the right shelves, deciding to throw out a few items he no longer wanted or needed, before making a lazy, simple but thoroughly enjoyable pasta dinner. He opened a bottle of red wine with his meal and enjoyed a second glass after eating while reading a book he had not managed to pick up for a few weeks and listening to a couple of his favourite CDs. He enjoyed his time thoroughly. The fact that he had not been able to read for some time brought it home to him just how busy he had been recently and that a day spent entirely on his own, doing everyday things, felt like the height of luxury. As he began to doze, laid out on the sofa, he felt warm and utterly, utterly relaxed.

By Monday morning, Guy felt entirely refreshed. Training went smoothly and the gradual progress he was making in his skills and relationships with team-mates improved. Grant kept himself to himself, which was fine by Guy for the time being. He left that day without staying for his extra, self-imposed training sessions, as he had a dentist's appointment for an introductory check-up.

The dentist was across town. Guy took a new route to get there, a short cut recommended by Reeves that would avoid some of Welby's busier roads. It took him into the industrial estate on the border of the town centre, a cluster of huge, imposing buildings, some old and dirty, some newer but still rather unattractive. There were several buildings that were derelict, ghost shells of industry that had long left the town, run-down shelters with broken windows and signs covered in pollution. It was a pretty grim place to be, but one that Guy realised had sustained Welby and its community for a long, long time.

He was on the road that took him out of the area when he saw a large group of people on the pavement ahead. They were standing outside a closed wrought-iron gate that led up to one of the larger warehouse units. As Guy got nearer, he saw some were holding placards, some had banners and none of them had particularly happy expressions on their faces. Guy guessed what was going on: he had found Cooper's Mill. These people were the strike team, showing their indignation at the job losses and removal of business from the area.

Guy pulled up at the side of the road. He had remembered what he had decided to do only days before in the players' bar – to provide the town of Welby with as much support in their hour of need as he could and if that meant off the pitch as well as on, he meant to do it.

He made a quick call on his mobile to the dentist to rearrange his appointment for later in the week, then got out of his car. He felt a little nervous, not entirely sure what he would say or do. He joined the crowd of men and women, deciding to mingle in to get a better idea of what exactly was going on. There were about a hundred or so picketers, showing their protest simply by being there. Near the gate he could see a small group of policemen who seemed to be there as much as a warning as anything else. No one took much notice of Guy at first. A couple of people glanced over at him. He guessed that no one had seen him park up down the road before joining them. In an attempt to ingratiate himself, he struck up a conversation with an older-looking man who stood on his own nearby.

"Hello there," Guy smiled. "How's it all going?"

"The support's strong. No doubt about that. But as for whether it'll make any difference, that's another thing. There've been negotiations going on for the past couple of days and the reports back aren't exactly promising." The man stopped and looked suspiciously at Guy.

"You a reporter, or summat?" he asked, disapprovingly. "You're not one of the workers with an accent like that."

Guy laughed. "No, not at all." He stuck out his hand. "My name's Guy Holbrook. I'm the new fly half for Welby."

The man took his hand. "Walter Davies. Don't follow sport much."

Guy was tickled by the man's honesty.

"You're probably a wiser man for it," he grinned.

"Well, I do know what the team means to this town. And it's good to see one of you down here showing some support."

"Hey, you!" The two men's introductions were suddenly interrupted by the sound of an enraged, gruff voice.

Guy looked across. He recognised the approaching owner of the voice immediately – Nutter Harris.

"You've got some bloody cheek showing your face round here. Are you taking the piss, or summat?" Harris growled, livid.

The nearest picketers turned to look at them. Guy heared someone laugh and shout out "Hey, Holbrook!"

"No, it's nothing like that. It's a good cause. I just wanted to show my support."

"Support! Get out of it!" Harris became sarcastic. "Not feeling so popular now that you've moved up North? Your agent sent you down here to do some public relations?"

"I'm afraid you've got it all wrong, Norman. I genuinely feel strongly about the strike..."

By this point, many had moved closer to the arguing men to get a better view.

"'Norman?'" Harris' voice rose in disbelief. "Nobody calls me 'Norman'. Not anyone who likes the look of their face, anyway."

Guy saw him clench his fists and steeled himself for the worst. He was about to try and calm the situation, when a commanding, but not angry voice boomed over him.

"Harris!" the voice demanded. "Leave it alone!"

The encroaching crowd parted, allowing a tall, broad-shouldered man to pass through.

"Now, what's this all about?" the man said imposingly.

"Bloody trouble-maker, that's what it's all about!" Nutter growled. The tall man gave Harris a disapproving look that dampened his fervour immediately. The man obviously had a lot of respect among the people around here.

"I was just passing," Guy attempted to explain what had happened. "I'd heard about the strike and I wanted to show my support for the cause."

"Don't give me that crap! You've no idea what this is all about. You're just some posh git who's never had to do a hard day's work in his life!" Harris' anger had apparently returned.

"Come on, Harris. Let's hear him out." The tall man commanded calm once more.

"I just thought I might be able to help out. I'm sorry. I didn't want to cause any trouble. Perhaps I should just leave..."

"I believe him." The old man who Guy had been speaking to earlier suddenly intervened. "He seems genuine enough. A nice young man all round."

"Yeah, Dad," the tall man shrugged. "I don't see any reason why we should mistrust him."

"But..." Harris began.

"Why don't you just take a walk around the block, Harris. Cool off a little." There was no threat or aggression in the man's voice and yet it was still arresting and persuasive. So persuasive that Harris did as he was told, albeit with a reluctance that was obvious in his swaggering movements and in the scowl he directed at Guy.

Now Harris was out of the way, the tall man extended a hand towards Guy.

"I'm Shaw Davies. Somehow, I've ended up as the co-ordinator of all this." Davies nodded behind him to the strike team, only a few of whom were paying any attention to the now much less noisy and interesting interaction. Shaw indicated the old man on his left. "This is my Dad."

"It's all right, son," the man intervened. "We've met already. He's one of the good ones, I can tell. None of the local lads on the team have turned up like he did, have they? No, his heart's in the right place, and no mistaking."

Guy felt bashful at the praise. "Thanks," he smiled, sheepishly. "I'm Guy. Guy Holbrook. I play for..."

Shaw laughed. "Yeah, I know. It was a good match Saturday. A lot better than your first one!"

"Tell me about it!" Guy agreed. "But I'm settling in more now. The only way is up from now on!"

Guy took his first good look at Davies. The man was around six-foot-four and his body, although not overly muscular, looked well-built, as if exercised and developed by manual work. He wore a dark jumper, jeans that defined his thick legs and a pair of large leather boots. He had chestnut-brown hair, cropped at the sides and ruffled and messy on top in a natural-looking style. His face had large but attractive features, a prominent nose, ears that stuck out and gave his face a cheeky quality and large, hooded eyes that would have appeared almost sleepy if it wasn't for their bright intelligence and piercing green colour. Guy was suddenly struck by how handsome his new friend was and, overcoming the quickening of his pulse, forced himself to speak.

"I'm sorry about all this. I should've tried to get in touch before I came down. Perhaps I ought to leave... come back at a more appropriate time."

Leaving was actually the last thing he wanted to do. What he really desired was to spend a lot more time in Shaw's presence.

"No, No. Don't do that." Shaw shook his head. "Like Dad, I'm glad to see you here. It is good to see some support coming from outside the work force. And someone so important to the town, someone in the public eye like you."

Davies paused, looking directly into Guy's eyes as he rubbed the stubble on his chin. Guy became momentarily distracted by the attractiveness of the unconventionally handsome man. Suddenly, Davies winked, his thoughtful face breaking into an incredibly appealing grin. Guy's heart skipped a beat at the sudden familiarity.

"I think you should definitely stick around, Guy," Davies gently but firmly placed one of his large arms around Guy's shoulders, causing a shiver of arousal to run down Guy's spine. "I think I've come up with a way to use you."

At that moment Guy could only revel inwardly at the possibilities of Shaw's veiled meaning. Feeling almost dizzy at the sudden onrush of desire, he replied with an equally laden retort.

"Use me any way you like, Shaw. Any way at all."

He looked up at the gorgeous man wrapped round him, feeling happier by the second that he had decided to give the strike a go.

Shaw's idea was a good one. Over the course of the strike, he had made contacts in the local press, and he gave a couple of the ones who had shown sympathy to the workers' cause a call, offering them first stab at the story of the new Welby player who was showing his support. Within an hour, a reporter from *The Welby Gazette* had arrived, followed shortly after by a news crew from the region's television station. They both interviewed Guy in turn and he tried to put over his concern about the impending loss of jobs for the local factory workers in an honest, yet emphatic way, stressing how the withdrawal of industry would affect Welby's economy in the future.

After the interviews were over, the camera crew stayed to get shots of the crowd, and to film the interviewer's report on the afternoon and the strike. Guy hung around for a while. Shaw introduced him to many of the strikers, who were, unlike Harris, pleased to see him. Not all recognised him at first, but when they knew who he was and where he was from, they were obviously glad to have him onboard. Through the afternoon, Guy felt increasingly useful and his eagerness to aid the strikers grew and grew. Before he left, he had a long talk with Shaw about what was organised for the upcoming week, enthusing at how keen he was to involve himself further in what would happen. He assured Shaw he would try to get other Welby team members down to the factory to help out. The two men exchanged numbers and Guy's less altruistic interest in Shaw suddenly rekindled. The swapping of means of contact with a handsome guy was something Guy usually did with other motives and he caught himself – the afternoon's events were about Welby. However, as Shaw's handsome face beamed a goodbye at him and he gripped Guy tenderly but firmly on his shoulder, the attraction grew once more and Guy hoped that his dual interest in the man would intertwine with time.

Later, at home, Guy caught his interview on the local news. What he said wasn't featured heavily – only a few sentences were used, but the piece was one of the main stories on the show and there were many shots of the strikers and Guy talking. He felt that he came across well, his worry that he may have seemed a little condescending or patronising being totally allayed. The main thing was that appropriate attention had been drawn to the strike and, though Guy was unsure just how much what he had done would affect the overall outcome, that evening he felt happy just to have made a first step. To top it all, Lambert rang him to congratulate him.

"I realise you didn't do it for your own publicity or for the team's," the manager told Guy. "At the same time, it's hardly going to do any damage, is it? I'm sure it'll help iron out the rest of those teething problems you had with settling in."

Guy felt like a studious pupil getting praise from a favourite teacher.

"And it's good to know at least one of you guys has got a heart. Your mind's not only on mucking about with a load of hairy-arsed blokes," Lambert said, somewhat sternly.

"Not all the time," Guy acquiesced, smiling inwardly.

"Anyway, just thought I'd let you know what good work you did today. Well done."

"Thanks, boss."

"Right, I'd best be off. Got a bit of a business dinner with some suits from one of the sponsors."

"Drink the bar dry, Ron," Guy joked. "I'll see you tomorrow."

Lambert was laughing as he hung up.

Guy was feeling very glad that he had decided to help out that afternoon and even happier that he had not been intimidated by what Harris had said to him and left without his appearance having any consequence. Using his celebrity and public position in such a way made him feel he was doing something really worthwhile. He thought back to his job in London and how, on many days there, he had felt as if he was wasting his life. Now, with his body and physical abilities engaged regularly on the pitch and becoming emotionally and socially involved in a community that accepted and needed him, his life felt amazingly full in comparison. He had a relaxing, calm-filled evening and went to bed early to prepare himself for the challenge of a new and exciting day.

Eight

Arriving in the locker room the next morning, Guy was greeted more warmly by his team-mates. Save Grant, whose miserable countenance was immovable as usual, there was none of the animosity or standoffishness that Guy had felt in his first few weeks. It appeared that many of the men had seen or read about his appearance at the factory the day before and those who hadn't had heard about it on their arrival that morning. The general atmosphere was one of approval and in many cases, admiration. Guy was asked several times by different people about the strike and three of his team-mates offered their time to him, saying the next time he went down they would join him to help out. Gripper Mason was especially attentive and the two men had their first proper conversation since Guy's arrival. Mason, usually a monosyllabic, gruff man, was that morning quite the chatterbox. It transpired that he had two brothers in good positions at Cooper's Mill who had been working there many years and who were now about to lose their livelihood. It had not occurred to Mason that, as a minor celebrity in the town, he could raise public interest in the strike. Having been inspired by Guy's actions the previous day, he had decided to get involved and do what he could. Guy gave him and the other men who showed an interest Shaw Davies' contact number, provisionally arranging a trip to the factory on the following Thursday after practice.

Kyle also collared Guy for a chat. He, too, was pleased with Guy for what he had done at Cooper's Mill, but had something else on his mind.

"It was very good of you, Guy. I wish I had thought of doing something like that for them," he said as they changed into their kit. He was almost naked, only a pair of white Y-fronts between him and complete nudity. "There was only one thing wrong with it, though."

Guy eyed him with concern. Only one person so far had criticised him for his involvement in the strike and that was Nutter Harris. His concern quickly dissipated, however, as Kyle slid his underwear down and continued.

"It meant you missed a training session." He winked, pulling his shorts from his bag. "I was ready and raring to go, as well."

Making sure that none of the other men around were paying attention, Guy flicked a glance downwards to Kyle's crotch. "You're a big boy, Kyle," he said, wryly. "I'm sure you could manage a good session by yourself."

Kyle stepped into his shorts, pulled them up and jiggled his sizeable packet inside. "It's never the same as when you're with someone else, though, is it?"

"No, it isn't," Guy agreed. "And we've got the team to think of, haven't we?"

Kyle looked puzzled. "You what?" he asked.

"It was..." Guy lowered his voice and sat down next to Kyle. "It was just an idea I had. The game we played on Saturday was a lot better than we've played before, wasn't it?"

Kyle nodded.

"Well, it set my mind going. It improved... *we* improved because we've become a lot closer, I'm sure of it. And I think the main reason for that was..."

"Last week's training?" Kyle interrupted. He raised his eyebrows as if he was giving the idea some serious thought. "I like your way of thinking. And if it means we can try and improve some more, all the better."

Guy chuckled. "See me later," he said. "I'll see what I can do."

After Reeves had finished with them for the day, Kyle and Guy went to the gym as they had done the week before to do some extra weight training. Gripper Mason joined them. Mason apparently was taking a new shine to Guy as a result of the support he had shown at the Mill and became increasingly approachable throughout the day. He showed his first genuine, non-rugby related interest in Welby's new player and Guy was extremely appreciative of the chance to bond with another team-mate. Gripper, despite his gruff exterior, was actually a level-headed and friendly man with a dry sense of humour that frequently broke through his brusque exterior. To Guy's surprise, they chatted about each other's lives and histories as they trained and both found each other worthy of the curiosity.

Gripper had had a variety of jobs before Welby had taken him on full time, the longest lasting and most affecting of which had been bouncer work in a city not so far away. The work had been tough, not so much because of the fights and trouble that he had to face, but because of the related crime. Many of the men he worked with were involved with drugs or with gangs, an area that he had wanted to steer well clear of. He had been about to quit, sick of the late nights, standing outside in the cold and the threats of serious violence when, thankfully, Welby offered him the chance to turn professional. He had never looked back, enjoying every moment of his sporting career to date.

Guy was incredibly glad to have the opportunity to see another side of Mason. It did, of course, restrict the kind of training he and Kyle really wanted to do, but at least it meant they got some serious extra exercise in before they were tempted to do anything else.

Eventually, however, the chance arose for them to be on their own.

"10... 11... 12!" Mason panted, dropping the arm of the bench press back into its starting position. "That's me done, lads. I'm all out. I'll have to leave you young 'uns to it."

He eased his mighty frame off the bench and stood up.

""Young 'uns!"" Guy laughed. "We're not so far behind you, you know!" He guessed that Mason was somewhere around thirty-five.

"Well, until you catch up, it's my right to be patronising! See you tomorrow!"

Mason left the room and Guy took his place on the machine, lying down so that his legs splayed either side.

"He's a good bloke, Mason," Kyle started, grinning. "Takes some time to get to know him, but he's worth knowing in the end."

Guy braced himself, gripping the arm of the bench press with both hands.

"Still, glad he's gone, though," Kyle continued under his breath. He playfully placed a hand between Guy's legs, cupping his balls and splitting his arse cheeks with a couple of fingers. The caress felt lovely.

"I see what you mean," Guy said. In reciprocation, he grabbed at Kyle's shorts, taking a good handful of the mound within. Kyle was semi-hard already and his warm, gradually thickening piece beat thrillingly a couple of times against Guy's fingers. "But let's wait a while. Do a few more reps in here until Mason's gone. I feel like doing our extra training in the showers."

Kyle put his head on one side and raised his eyebrows in surprise.

"I hadn't thought of that," he said, removing his hand.

"These things come with practice," Guy reassured him, jokily, as he pushed upwards for his first repetition.

"Yeah, I think he's gone now," Kyle said as he took a good look around the changing rooms.

The two men had waited about fifteen minutes to give Mason enough time to shower and change, before finishing in the gym so they could move on to more pleasantly physical matters.

"Right," said Guy firmly. "Kit off, then we'll get in there. Get soaped up and see what happens."

Neither he nor Kyle took much time over getting undressed, both men whipping their sports gear off quickly and leaving it in a pile on the bench beside them. Guy's body felt overheated by exercise and the sensation of his sweat drying in the air, combined with the anticipation of what was about to happen, aroused him. He could feel his dick becoming engorged, not so that it was fully hard, but definitely so that it bounced a little less independently along with the movements of his body.

"Looks nice," Kyle complimented. "Can't wait to see it in action again."

"Same here." Guy reached across and gave the end of Kyle's member a playful tweak. "Got any shower gel?"

Kyle reached in his sports bag and took out a bottle of gel. He spun it around in the air with one hand.

"Come on, then, "Guy headed off to the showers. "Let's get clean."

"That's funny, mate," Kyle retorted as he followed behind. "I was in a good mind to get dirty!"

Guy stepped into the shower and pressed the button to turn on the hot water. It shot out over him, massaging his head and neck, pummelling the tired muscles of his shoulders and chest. It felt fantastic after the day's workout and he closed his eyes for a few seconds to bask in the pleasure. Before long, he felt two soapy hands at his back, tenderly pressing against his skin.

"That's nice, Kyle," he murmured as the hands ran over him. They gradually made their way downwards to his buttocks, firmly gripping and squeezing them. Then, he felt a blob of gel drop at the top of his bum cleavage and begin to ease its way down his crack. The sensation was exquisite and was followed by that of an inquisitive hand, spreading the gel over his skin, tickling it over his ringpiece.

"Been looking forward to getting back up there for days," Kyle murmured into Guy's ear. Kyle moved closer so that their bodies touched completely, his slippery hands sliding over Guy's midriff, down his belly to his thighs. Guy could feel just how eager Kyle was. A hot length pressed against his back, slowly rubbing up and down against him. It felt good, very good, but Guy wasn't about to get things over quickly.

"Easy, tiger." He turned round. "You won't be getting in there that soon."

Both men were fully erect now. Guy positioned himself so the end of his penis touched Kyle's and with subtle, small movements he pleasured them both by rubbing the two pricks against each other just around the tip.

"Oh no?" Kyle asked. "And what have I got to wait around for?"

He squeezed out some more shower gel, this time directly onto Guy's prick. The gel was cold, but very pleasant, and the large blob dripped over the sides onto the tiles of the shower. Kyle grabbed hold of Guy's dong, smearing the gel over it, making sure the entire thing was covered in the slippery substance. He pulled on Guy's skin a couple of times, then slid his fingers over its length, rubbing and tickling the end with particular attention.

Guy puffed with desire, as his need to bring himself to orgasm as quickly as he could grew with every caress. But he still intended to make the session last a bit longer.

"I don't know," he winced, pulling himself out of Kyle's grasp. "I just like the idea of teasing you a little."

"Is that right? I'll show you teasing!" Good-naturedly, Kyle suddenly took Guy in a strong bear hug. He yanked his buddy to one side, almost unbalancing him, then planted a ferocious kiss on his lips. Guy reciprocated, taken somewhat aback. He realised Kyle was playing around, but, at the same time, was rather turned on by the fervent passion of his friend. He could feel a finger at his backside again, tracing the remnants of the shower gel and making its first attempts at insertion. Guy's heart was pounding, his intentions to take things slower all but abandoned as a result of his friend's animal, enthusiastic behaviour. The thought of being taken, fast and hard right there, was undeniably attractive, and he turned around, bent over and split his cheeks for Kyle.

"What the bloody hell's going on here?" a loud, manly voice interrupted.

Shocked, Guy and Kyle quickly disentangled themselves. So speedily, in fact that Guy slipped slightly on the soapy floor, bumping into the wall. He covered himself with his hands, but knew his hard-on had been well and truly exposed.

"Mason!" exclaimed Kyle, who was having similar trouble hiding his erection. "I thought you'd left!"

"Apparently so! Enjoying yourselves, were you?" Mason looked thunderous.

Guy felt incredibly embarrassed. "We were just playing about. You know, lads' stuff," he said, trying to explain.

To his further surprise, Mason suddenly grinned. "You pair of idiots!" he laughed. "You should have seen your faces when I turned the corner. And the sight of you now. It's a right picture."

Guy looked over at Kyle who was sheepishly shuffling his feet, his hands still over his crotch.

"You just ought to be glad it was me who found you and not one of the other guys," Mason continued. He positioned himself under one of the shower nozzles and turned it on. "Feeling horny, were you? I can remember what it was like at your age. You'll stick it in anything that moves. Not that it gets any better when you're my age either!" he chuckled.

Relaxing into the situation, Guy uncovered his cock. Although the strength of his erection had lessened from the shock, it was still extended more than it would be at complete rest. He eyed Mason's naked body. Mason was a huge man, with large arms and shoulders and a bulky chest decorated with dark hair. He had a sizeable belly on him, not one that was blubbery or loose, but one that looked tight and that fit well on a man of his build. He was attractive in the extreme, not a conventional physical beauty, but masculine and powerful. Guy wouldn't have needed asking twice if Mason had come on to him. He had an idea. Maybe Mason, if the idea was put to him correctly, would be interested in one of his and Kyle's special training sessions. After all, he seemed to be at ease with the state in which he had found them.

"Well, it wasn't just that we felt a bit... you know, playful," Guy began as he began to wash himself down with water. "We had an ulterior motive."

Mason looked at him quizzically. "Oh, yeah?" he asked. "And what would that be?"

"We've done it before. Mucking about last week after training. And you know how much we improved in the game on Saturday?"

Mason shrugged in agreement.

"Well, I figured that it was connected. I mean, that because me and Kyle had got to know each other that much better we became more in tune with each other on the pitch."

Mason looked thoughtful. "Could be true. It makes as much sense as some of the exercises that Reevesy has us doing day in day out." And then, realising that Guy was implying something else, he quickly asked, "Are you suggesting what I think you're suggesting?"

As Kyle nudged him to shut him up, Guy put on his best look of unthreatening friendliness. "I think so. Are you up for it?"

Again, Mason spent a few seconds deep in thought. Then he turned, his stance one of complete openness.

"Fuck it. I'll try anything once. And if it's all for the cause of Welby, it'll be well worth doing."

"Oh, it'll be well worth doing, all right," Guy took a couple of steps towards him.

"So, what do you guys get up to in these situations?" Mason inquired innocently.

"Follow my lead, Grip," encouraged Guy. "I'm sure you'll pick it up in no time."

Mason had a stubby, thick-looking dick dangling out of a bush of light-brown pubes. Guy reached over and took hold of it. It was nice and warm to the touch, and it twitched a little as Guy pulled on it.

"Do you want me to do the same to you?" Mason asked, in between murmurs of pleasure.

"Why not?" Guy acquiesced. His own prick was filling once more as he thrilled at the chance of getting his hands on another man's genitals.

Mason grabbed it in one of his hefty paws and gave it a few yanks. Guy shivered at the touch, revelling in the sight of the beefy man becoming more and more involved in the sexual act. Mason looked fantastic, excited and active, a real man with real needs. Guy intended seeing to them.

"Looks like fun," Kyle had made his way over to the two men. "Any chance I can have a go?"

"I don't see why not," Mason shrugged. Without prompting from Guy, Mason took hold of Kyle's now fully-erect penis with his free hand.

"You're a fast learner," Kyle winced, closing his eyes with joy. Kyle traced his fingers along one of Mason's large, meaty thighs, stroked the inside of the top of his leg and then cupped the man's hefty, hairy balls. He began to play with them, massaging the skin, tickling them then pulling on them, not hard, just in a manner that would provide a variety of delicious sensations to their owner.

Mason's knob had become fully engorged. It was hardly the longest penis Guy had ever seen, but it was good and thick and took up a good deal of Guy's grasp. It looked rude and manly, throbbing away in Guy's clutch, and its head, a bright-pink colour, was temptingly suckable. Guy caught Mason's glance a couple of times as the three men masturbated each other. Mason grinned back at him each time, obviously more than happy to be doing what he was doing. After a couple of minutes, Guy moved in closer to his new sex buddy, wrapping one of his thighs around one of Mason's mighty legs. The warmth of the solid skin upon Guy's inner thigh felt fantastic. He positioned himself so that his balls dangled and beat delightfully against Mason's quads.

"So this is why they call you Gripper!" Kyle joked, indicating how Mason now had a dick firmly clenched in each hand.

"I wish it was!" chuckled Mason. "This is great stuff! And you know what? I feel closer to you two already."

"Told you it would work," panted Guy. He eased himself backwards off Mason's leg. "I've got a way to make us feel even closer, as well."

"What's that?" Mason asked, naively.

Guy sank down and crouched on the tiled floor. He took hold of Mason's member at its base with his right hand and looked up into Mason's expectant eyes. Guy opened his mouth slowly, then pushed his head forward, taking the very end of Mason's thick meat inside him. Mason's glans was enjoyably bulbous on Guy's tongue and against his lips and he took more of the length in. He could hear Mason swear with pleasure as he tasted the first sticky drops of his team-mate's juices, swallowing them down with abandon.

"Fucking hell, Holbrook," Mason sighed. "I don't care if it improves my game any more. Just carry on doing it!"

With that encouragement, Guy pushed himself further onto the piece. The mass of curly light-brown pubes tickled his nose and mouth. Mason was almost fully in him now. He sucked up and down the length a couple of times, mouth-wanking his friend, then relaxed his gullet as much as he could and pushed himself totally onto the thing. Mason moaned loudly as Guy swallowed, writhed his tongue and twitched his head from side to side to stimulate the cock inside him. His nose and lips were pressed fully into Mason's bush and the chunky muscle felt great filling his mouth and throat. He pulled back to give the length a series of good, hard pounding sucks, then removed himself completely from it. He studied the cock for a few seconds, loving how it looked all engorged and covered with his own drool, then looked upwards. Mason and Kyle were close together now, each with an arm around each other. Kyle's erection rested gently on Mason's belly, beating upwards a couple of times then back onto the skin with arousal. He and Mason had obviously been enjoying the sight of Guy munching away on a hard prick. Guy was enjoying it immensely, but didn't want to be the only one working it.

"Come on, Kyle," he beckoned his friend down. "Don't be lazy. Give me some assistance here."

Kyle crouched so that he was at eye level with Guy. "Well, I suppose if we're going to initiate someone into our gang properly, it would be better if all the founder members were involved," he joked.

"Very funny. Put this in your mouth," Guy ordered. He directed Mason's penis towards Kyle's waiting mouth and Kyle took it inside without protest. Just as Guy had done moments before, Kyle began sucking on Mason's piece. The sight was delicious – a close-up view of a horny hunk munching away on a steely, veined love-rod. Action in the flesh like that was better than any pornography Guy had seen: there was no distance between what was happening and himself. He was involved in the joyous, exciting orgy right there and then.

He came out of his reverie and got stuck in again. He brushed the side of Kyle's face with his lips. The two men's heads remained close as they began to take turns on Mason's length, one of them sucking for a few moments, then the other. Their tongues met over the end as they licked away, French-kissing each other as they blowjobbed at the same time. Guy positioned himself at one side of the erection. Kyle followed his lead and the two men rubbed their lips up and down the length, their mouths making a stimulating loop. Guy thrilled at taking his pleasure alongside Kyle. It appealed on so many levels. He here was, doing something usually only shared between two people, and there was someone else involved, watching him and involved with him in the glorious acts. It felt dirty, but oh, so good. The viewpoint of voyeurism, seeing his buddies in the throes of sexual excitement so close to him, only added to his enjoyment. Here was Kyle, the man who he had introduced into the world of gay sex only days before, continuing his explorations with another newcomer, both men extremely attractive in their own way and both greatly happy to be doing what they were doing. But most of all, what excited Guy as he and Kyle sucked away at Mason was the dynamic of subordination. Mason was a huge, masculine man, older than both Kyle and himself. That they were concentrating on pleasuring him rather than themselves at that moment thrilled Guy in the extreme and his cock throbbed away with sheer joy.

Guy shivered as he suddenly felt Kyle's hands on his bouncing dick, giving it a few wanks, dipping down between his extended thighs and cupping and squeezing his balls. He reciprocated, feeling his way up Kyle's thighs, then grabbing hold of the protruding bits between them. The three men were joined once more in sexual pleasure, each one having direct contact with each other and, for a minute or two, Guy felt completely lost, not wanting anything else from the world but for that moment to last forever. Eventually, the perfection of the mutual joy was broken as Mason placed a hefty hand on each of his friends' heads, slipped his hips backwards and withdrew his penis from their reach.

"Bloody fantastic, boys!" he growled, eyes half-shut with ecstasy. "But what I fancy now is a good rut. Can either of you oblige?"

Mason wiped the sweat from his brow. Some of the curls of his mop of hair had stuck to his forehead. Guy laughed at how attractive he looked, all worked up and red-faced like that.

"Got the picture now, Mason, haven't we?" Kyle smiled. He gave Mason's hefty backside a whack with one of his hands, then pointed over at Guy with a flick of his thumb. "I think Guy's your man for that kind of thing. The bastard loves it up him."

Guy shrugged in a what-can-I-say manner. Kyle stood up and moved to his side, then placed his hands on his shoulders, his prick bouncing at Guy's neck.

"And I can seriously recommend being up there. Tried it the other day, Mason. It was the best fuck I'd had in a long time."

"I try my best," sighed Guy with good-humoured modesty, before placing a brief kiss upon the shaft of Kyle's dick.

"Learnt quite a lot as well, I can tell you," Kyle continued. "Like there's something we can do to make sure everything goes smoothly."

Kyle put his hands under Guy's armpits and lifted him slightly. Guy followed the direction and stood up.

"Turn around," Kyle told him. "And show us two that gorgeous arse of yours."

Guy did as he was told, bending over, then reaching behind himself to split his cheeks with his hands. The position felt delightfully rude, having two men look at his arsehole like that, and tingles of joy spread over his body.

"Looks good, doesn't it?" Guy heard Kyle say behind him. He felt a hand take a good squeeze of his butt.

"Not half," agreed Mason. "Never seen a fellah like that before. But I'm telling you, I'm bursting to get up that tight little hole."

"Hold your horses," Kyle told him. "Like I said, there's a little preparation yet."

Guy felt a finger trace around his anus. He took in a sharp breath at the sudden pressure on the tender nerve endings, then another as a wet blob, which he guessed was spit from Kyle's mouth, dropped onto his backside at the top of his split crack, then gradually oozed downwards to where the finger still applied pressure. Having caught the makeshift lube, Guy felt the finger slip and tickle around his hole again, this time with much more ease, before it made its first confident probe. Guy concentrated on relaxing his muscles to allow the digit to enter him. The first intrusion pushed against his tautness, but the friction felt great as it poked fully inside.

"It's bloody tight!" said Kyle. "I hope you'll be squeezing away at Mason's cock the way you are on my finger!"

"Damn right I will," murmured Guy confidently. He couldn't wait to get something larger up there.

"You have a feel," Kyle encouraged Mason. "Try it before you buy it."

Guy felt the finger exit him, then just as his rectum closed up once more, another replaced it, this time slipping up him with much more ease.

"Fucking hell, I see what you mean," Mason exclaimed, giving Guy a couple of frigs as he spoke. "Oh, mate. Are you ready for a bit of this yet?"

Guy felt something hot and hard slap against his butt. He guessed it was Mason's member. He wanted it up him more than anything and he turned eagerly to look at Kyle.

"Get the johnnies and the lube. They're in my jacket pocket." Guy watched his buddy jog out of the shower, then checked out what Mason was doing. The man smiled at Guy before easing his hips back and forth so that his cock rubbed over the skin of his backside, his finger matching the rhythm perfectly. The view was fantastic and only got better with Kyle's return, naked and erect, and carrying the tools of the trade.

"Here we go," said Kyle, eagerly. "Let's get some of this on him."

Guy turned away as he heard the rip of a lube packet, then felt the squelchy fluid drop onto his arsehole. Where there was only one, there were suddenly two men at him and he could feel two hands playing with his arse, two fingers being inserted inside him and two hot pricks rubbing over his cheeks. He felt fantastic being the plaything of two hunks like that and soon enough he was ready for much more.

"Come on, Mason," he pleaded eventually. "Let's take it to the next stage."

"Horny little fucker, aren't you?" Mason asked as he rubbered up.

And then, to Guy's relief, he felt the two strong arms of Gripper Mason take hold of him at the waist and firmly position him before the man's hot piece, as he searched for the inviting entrance. It took a couple of tries at first. Mason aimed too high, then too low, and then he found it and Guy felt the man slid slowly up him.

"Perfect fucking fit," Mason groaned as he shoved himself fully inside.

Guy felt the man settle himself before his first stroke, and he took a moment to enjoy the sensation of Mason's warm skin upon him, the mighty belly that rested on his back and most of all, the wonderful happiness of being filled from behind. And then the first shunt came, a slow drag out, then a firm pump back in, like the initial movements of some great piece of steam-driven machinery. It was quickly followed by another, then another, steady pumps that invaded Guy with an eager, demanding sureness. They hurt Guy all right, but what a pain, what a beautifully exquisite pain. Wanting more of it, he started to push himself backwards to meet Mason's thrusts. The fucks gained in friction, and reached deeper inside him as he and Mason achieved a regular, thrilling rhythm. Gradually, Guy's pain began to subside, but not completely – he didn't want that. To him, it was the ultimate physical indicator of what was happening to him, that he was being taken by a man, that he was experiencing a man at his rawest and most bestial, getting fucked, hard and rough, so he never wanted the pain to disappear fully. But the pain had been taken over and dominated by the new and warming pleasure of secret, inner, recently relaxed skin being stretched and pummelled by the *ne plus ultra* of male body parts.

"How's that, Holbrook?" Mason asked, panting.

Guy closed his eyes to concentrate on what was happening up him. "Oh, it's good, Grip. It's really fucking good."

"It looks good as well," added Kyle.

In his reveries, Guy had almost forgotten that there was anyone else involved apart from himself and Mason. The realisation that Kyle was watching him get fucked in the arse by a big bruiser of a man made him feel pleasantly sleazy and even more aroused.

"Anything you can do to help me out?" Kyle asked.

"I'm sure there's something I could think of. Come round here." Guy waved Kyle around to the front of him so that Kyle's erection pointed directly at Guy's face.

"And you definitely look like you need some help," Guy winced. He grabbed hold of Kyle's meat, leaned over a little, then took it into his mouth. It was sticky and he could taste Kyle's arousal, but that moment wasn't one for the subtle pleasures of lovemaking – it was for the harder, more energetic delights of abandoned shagging. Guy took Kyle by the hips and dragged him in and out a couple of times, indicating what he wanted his buddy to do. Kyle cottoned on immediately and began to screw Guy in the mouth, not as fast as the speed Mason had reached behind him, but at a good, forceful pace. Guy was luxuriant. Here he was, being fucked at both ends by two fantastic specimens of mankind, his orifices filled and exited again and again by some truly wonderful man-meat. It felt fantastic. The part of his soul that cried out for the physical affection of another man was being comforted, succoured, satiated. It was utter, utter bliss. Every pound inwards shook his body and being, lifted him to heights of pleasure where he felt dizzy with happiness. He never wanted it to end, the three men's groans making a deep, grunted chorus of lust, the smell of their sweat and sex a perfume of fulfilled desire. But, of course, it had to. As the rough touch of Gripper Mason's right hand reached around his body to yank on his dick, Guy knew that he was close to coming.

"You're gonna bring me off, Guy," Mason moaned. "Oh Guy, are you gonna bring me off."

Mason was shafting Guy very hard and very fast. Just as it was getting too much, Guy heard Mason give a cry which he recognised as that of a man releasing his load. He felt Mason's body stiffen as the man gave him a good, hard fuck, dragging him back fully onto the rigid length, and then relax as the shafting continued, slower and much less furious. Guy's attention shifted as once more he heard a cry, this time from Kyle. Kyle's pumps increased in speed, and Guy felt the thing in his mouth become unbelievably hard, before a hot load flew from it, coating the inside of his cheeks and tongue. The cock throbbed away repeatedly, spewing shot after shot of salty fluid, and Guy swallowed it down gluttonously. The taste and heat of it thrilled him and almost before he knew it, he too was at the brink of orgasm, thanks to the able hand of Mason. Guy's entire body became stiff as the tension built up in him, then as the fist on his dick shook away at him, the first of his spunk loads let fly. Yelling out with pleasure, he felt the come splash up onto his stomach as his member shuddered again and again. His rectum convulsed against the still-hard protuberance within it, grasping it tighter and tighter as the release of his sperm possessed him entirely. It was a great end to a great sex session. Guy could not have asked for anything more from it and, as the afterglow drifted over his body, like waves on the beach, he felt satisfied in a way he knew he wouldn't forget in a long time.

Guy stood up as Mason finally pulled out of him. Both his sex partners looked slightly dazed from their heady exertions, but they both smiled as Guy caught their eyes.

"Now I see why you two have been staying so late after training!" Mason exclaimed, his body still heaving as he tried to get his breath back. He pulled the condom off his flaccid cock, which, when revealed, was pleasantly shiny with his own come.

"Yeah, it's not time that shows up on your pay packet," laughed Kyle. "But it still seems worth it."

"You're telling me," said Mason. "That was the best fuck I've had in years!"

Guy had never imagined in a million years when he had arrived at Welby that he would find himself in such a situation with his two friends, let alone hear them talking about gay sex the way they were. He couldn't help breaking into a broad grin.

"What you grinning at?" Mason asked, in a tone that was much more like his regular, gruff self than Guy had seen since they become intimate.

"Oh, nothing," Guy broke off his daydreamy train of thought. He hit the button for the showers once more. "Just thinking how much I'd like to wash your back down for you, that's all!"

Nine

The following day, the training session went well. Reeves was stepping up the pace a little, as if their improvements of late had indicated to the coach that the team had much more in them and that he should push them further to tap into their inner potential. Guy enjoyed the challenge. He could feel himself tiring a little more than he had in a long time and stretching his body further than he had. On an individual and personal level, the training made him aware of his capabilities, that he could and wanted to do much more on the pitch. There were new insights Guy learnt from other team-mates as well that day. His moves when working with both Kyle and Mason seemed much slicker and refined than before. Again, it was as if a new understanding had been reached, or had increased between the players. Guy could also see the change, as well, when Kyle and Mason worked together. All three of them seemed to know each other and how their bodies moved, much better. Again, he wasn't the only one to notice the difference. Mason collared Guy after the day was over and the team were walking back inside to get changed.

"Only bloody works, doesn't it?" Mason said, ruffling Guy's hair with a playful, heavy-handed touch.

"I told you so. And it's a lot more fun than doing some extra lat pull downs, isn't it?

Mason leaned in closer as the two men entered the changing rooms. "I'll tell you what. We could do with getting a few of the other lads in on it. You know, improve their game as well."

Guy shrugged. He realised it was a good idea in theory, but had no thoughts on how to put it into practice.

"Maybe..." he began, peeling off his sweat-ridden shirt.

"Leave it to me," Mason reassured him with a confident nod. "I know these men better than you. There are at least one or two who wouldn't mind improving their game like we have. I'll drop a few hints, try and get them involved."

Mason walked off to a bench further away where his bag and clothes lay. Guy was suddenly intrigued. Which of his team-mates was Mason talking about? Was the man just making errors of judgement or was he as clued up as he made out? Guy hoped it was the latter as it would mean two important things: the further development of Welby's game and one hell of a shag that would lead the players to that point.

Later in the week, Guy arranged another visit to the strike site with Mason and a couple of others from the Welby team. Guy arrived first at the factory and, to his surprise and delight, received a round of applause from the strike team as he walked up to them. People shook his hand and patted him on the back as he made his way through the crowd and he returned their friendly interest with smiles and brief conversation. Eventually, he heard someone call his name and he turned to find Shaw Davies walking towards him.

"Guy! Glad you could make it." Davies wore a genuine smile that made his face look mind-blowingly handsome.

"And I'm glad to be here." Guy felt his insides tremble at the sheer impact of being in Davies' presence. "Very glad."

"Looks like people are pleased you got the strike on TV last week," Davies said as he glanced around.

"Yeah, I wasn't expecting such a response," Guy laughed. "Not that I'm complaining."

He thought back to the time in the players' bar after his first match. A friendly welcome from the general populace of Welby hadn't seemed much of a possibility back then.

"Like I said on the phone, it was good coverage. And that's worth its weight in gold to us at the moment," Davies voice sounded grave and thoughtful.

"Well, anything to oblige you guys. I've got to confess, it didn't seem like much. It wasn't exactly hard work, just like part of the job for me. It's nothing to what the real strikers must be going through."

Guy realised that he had absolutely no experience behind him that matched that of the people on strike and that, especially in the relatively comfortable position he was in at the moment, he could only offer sympathy.

Davies placed a firm hand on Guy's shoulder and gave it a comforting squeeze.

"No, you're right, it's not. But that doesn't mean that what you did wasn't important. This battle is psychological as much as anything. When people give up, when they start dropping out, that's when we've lost the fight. What you did was give us something to lift our spirits. Can't you see how people have changed since last week? They're positive now. They've got hope that something will come of it all."

Guy looked deep into Davies' eyes. Even though he had only known the man a short while and this was only their second meeting, he had developed some deep feelings for him. Davies had a striking, powerful integrity and Guy respected him greatly for it. That Davies believed in himself to such a degree and had such a deep-seated need to help others was admirable in the extreme. Guy had been almost instantly taken with the arresting nature of his personality: the strong words spoken with confidence, his assured, non-arrogant manner, his clear, quick-thinking mind imbued with savvy developed from simply living a full and rich life, were all impressive and rather attractive qualities. That Davies' characteristics came in such a physically appealing package made Guy's feelings for him all the stronger.

Guy realised that what he was experiencing was something far more than sexual attraction. Something about just being around Davies moved him deep inside to the point where he wondered if it was reflected in his facial expressions or the way he spoke to the man. He had seen no signs of reciprocal feelings in Davies as yet and so didn't want to act on them. All he could do was to hope something would develop in his new friend and, until that point, wait and simply enjoy the rollercoaster ride of emotions he endured as a result of Davies being in his life.

Guy saw a familiar car park down the street not too far from his own. He recognised the driver immediately as Gripper Mason. Mason had arrived with Kyle in tow, who also wanted to boost morale for the workers. Both men walked towards Guy and Davies, smiling.

As the strikers had done with Guy when they noticed his arrival, they cheered at the sight of their two new recruits. Mason and Kyle raised their hands in appreciation, Mason winking and pointing at his brothers as he passed by.

"That was a warm welcome," Kyle beamed as he finally reached Guy. "I ought to come down more often."

"We're all very glad to see you two. As visitors go, it certainly makes a change from the coppers!" Shaw held out his hand, first to Kyle, then to Mason. "I'm Shaw. We spoke on the phone."

The three men made their introductions.

"Now, mate." Mason began, obviously wanting to get down to business straightaway. "What is it exactly that you want us to do here? Will it be the same as what happened with Guy here last week?"

"More or less," Shaw grinned, mysteriously. "Although we have upgraded a little."

"What do you mean?" asked Guy, feeling puzzled.

Shaw explained that, because there were more of Welby's players turning up that day, he had managed to get hold of some national, rather than local, press interest.

"Blimey!" exclaimed Mason. "I wish I'd worn a better shirt now!"

Suddenly, Shaw's mobile phone began to ring. He excused himself and, after a brief conversation, told the three rugby players that the television crew would be there soon. Sure enough, within the next ten minutes, a van with the familiar logo of a terrestrial TV station on the side arrived, accompanied by two new-looking cars. Guy recognised one of the newly arrived posse as the sports presenter from one of the most important news shows in the country. He had not realised the story would be so significant and felt a little nervous.

"Bloody hell!" Kyle had obviously also spotted the presenter. "Looks like we'll have to start talking like you, Guy," he joked. "This fellah might not understand our accents!"

Making sure that no one was watching, Guy gave Kyle a swift jab in the ribcage. "Behave yourself!" he said in a mock-motherly manner. "We want to look like the ultimate in solidarity in front of these guys."

"Excuse me a moment, will you, fellahs." Shaw began walking towards the crew. "I'd better see the lie of the land."

Guy watched Shaw as he entered into conversation with a couple of the crew. The man looked as confident and assured as ever and Guy felt appropriately mesmerised by the scene.

"Complex stuff, isn't it?" Mason asked, breaking Guy's thoughts momentarily. "All that equipment and people to organise. And I bet we'll only be on for a couple of minutes."

Guy was just thinking of how sublime a couple of minutes in the right situation with Shaw would be, when the sports reporter walked over to the three of them and introduced himself. The reporter gave a brief explanation of what would happen and a

147

rundown of what questions would be asked. It all seemed as straightforward to Guy as it had done with the local news crew, with the general process being more or less the same. He was definitely glad to have other people with him, however, as it did seem to take the pressure off having to perform and present himself to the camera to a large extent. The interview was run through off-camera to give the players a chance to work out what they would say and who would field which questions and then, when everyone was ready, it was filmed for real. It went pleasantly smoothly. Only Kyle stumbled over his words once and had to be given the chance to start his answer again. When the questions were over, shots of the men with the strikers themselves were taken, along with some of the surroundings and individual strikers with placards. Shaw was interviewed in front of the camera. Guy was glad about that as, coupled with the more serious questions the journalist asked, it indicated that the piece would not be just another sports piece, but show genuine interest in the strike itself. He felt rather elated when his involvement with the crew was over, as did both Kyle and Mason. It was the first time any of them had had that kind of interest shown in them outside their rugby playing and the fact that they had coped so well with it made them feel pleased with themselves. That they had also helped the strikers added to their satisfaction. They discussed their hopes for what might result from what they had done before they said goodbye to the strikers and left.

Later on, watching the news back in his flat, Guy found that his interpretation of the interview – that it was something more than just a sports piece – was correct. Although not one of the top stories, the piece was still in the main body of the news, rather than pigeonholed at the end with the rest of the sports stories. Guy felt that the right balance between the unusualness of the players' support for the strike and the presentation of the strikers' cause was achieved and he thought Shaw came across particularly well, seeming articulate and intelligent.

Right after the piece, his mother called.

"Those poor people!" she gasped, seemingly genuinely horrified. "No wonder you wanted to help!"

She started the conversation with a five-minute, non-stop monologue. She had obviously been quite excited at seeing her son on the national news and swept up by his involvement in the cause. She asked him more about what had started the strike (but not waiting for the answers), telling him how terrible it looked on the picket line and wondering what would happen next.

"I suppose it'll all be futile, though, won't it? The struggle?" She questioned with a genuine tinge of desperation in her voice.

"No one knows for sure," Guy told her. "We can only do what we can and hope for the best."

Guy knew that his mother's political savvy was actually quite limited and her involvement with or sympathy for any kind of direct activism had up to then been more or less non-existent. He guessed that she had been carried along by his part in the strike and the fact that it had all appeared on the national news.

"Well, is there anything I can do?" she asked.

Guy was grateful for her interest and glad that she had been affected, but still couldn't picture her with a protest sign in her hand, shouting at the managers as they drove past the workers into the factory.

"I'll tell them of your support. The more they know people are behind them, the better," Guy reassured her.

"Oh, how can they not be? I can just picture how I'd feel in the same situation. Dreadful, absolutely dreadful."

Guy knew that his mother, having luckily led a rather privileged life in economic terms, would actually have no idea what it would be like to be struck by redundancy in such a manner but, not wanting to undermine her enthusiasm, he agreed.

"Still, it looked like there might be some perks to getting involved." His mother was suddenly playful.

"What do you mean?" Guy hoped she wasn't about to put a politically naïve foot in it.

"That man, darling. He's quite a dreamboat, isn't he?"

Guy was gobsmacked. He thought his feelings for Shaw were hidden away and secret. His mother's comment made him feel as if they were exposed and obvious to all.

"Oh, you mean Shaw?" he said, trying to come across as nonchalant. "Yeah, he's a nice guy. Intelligent. A good organiser."

"You might add 'gorgeous' to your list. Anything happening there that I should know about?"

Guy wished there was. "No, not really. We're just friends."

His mother laughed. "Well, I'm sure you can work on it."

Again, Guy had the strange feeling that his emotions for Shaw had been sussed – in fact, he was sure they had been. His mother could often seem psychic when it came to matters of the heart, especially when they concerned her son.

"While we're on the subject," she continued. "Anything from Hugo lately?"

Hugo? Guy had become so wrapped up in what had been going on in Welby over the past couple of weeks that he had barely given his lackadaisical boyfriend a second thought.

"Erm..." he began, not really knowing what to say on the matter. "We've both been rather busy lately."

"The flames of passion dying a little, eh? Never mind, you're too young to get tied down, anyway, and Hugo never was the most reliable of men, was he?"

"I guess not." Guy knew that what his mother was saying was right, but there was still a slight twinge of sadness that, deep down, he knew that their relationship was over.

"But life's boat sails on, darling," his mother comforted him, then added, "Hopefully, on to better 'Shaws'."

Guy groaned. "I think I'd better go."

The two of them said their goodbyes and then Guy went into the kitchen to prepare his evening meal. It had been a good day, all in all. He felt proud of himself for what he had done for the strikers and pleased with his and his team-mates' appearance on national television. Only his burgeoning feelings for Shaw and the dying embers of his emotions for Hugo caused him any uncertainty. But he knew that in both areas it would be a case of wait and see and he managed to ease his mind almost completely and settle into a relaxing night in as the evening progressed.

Ten

The weekend arrived quickly and along with it another match. This time, the pressure was really on for Welby. The game was an important one, being part of the Cup tournament, and one that, if won, would bring both prestige and one step nearer to the Cup itself. It was an away match, due to be played in the nearby town of Hadcastle. Guy arrived at the Welby stadium that Saturday morning in good spirits but feeling more nervous than he had felt for a while. It was his first away game with Welby and that it was a rather significant one on top of that just added to his anxieties. He knew Hadcastle were a good team and one that would be hard to beat. Though wanting to face up to the challenge, he was fully aware of just what a challenge it would be.

A coach had been arranged. Boarding it, Guy began to feel a little better. His team-mates were in ebullient spirits, taking the mickey out of each other and, more often, the team they were about to face. They weren't exactly raucous (Guy guessed that they too had some trepidation about the match) but their lively behaviour worked to relax Guy somewhat and he joined in with their chants, songs and jokes. A couple of times, he caught Gripper Mason's eye, who winked at him with an assured confidence. Kyle, too, seemed, whenever Guy looked at him directly, to hold a certain poise, as if he had been bolstered internally by what had happened between them and felt prepared for what lay ahead. Guy took great succour from the two men. It almost felt as if the links between them had grown to the point where all three were telepathically linked on an emotional level and Guy just couldn't wait to discover how it would work out on the pitch.

Hadcastle was not far away from Welby. The journey took less than half an hour on the motorway. Guy knew Hadcastle to be a popular, successful side of the same level of fame and achievement as Welby. They had a similar amount of money behind them and Guy found their stadium and facilities to be of as high a quality as those at Welby. As he and his team-mates left the coach he was impressed, once again, by what League playing had to offer, to players and fans alike.

The team entered the changing rooms on arrival, wanting to ground themselves before the match. The changing rooms were obviously relatively new and up-to-date and extremely well-kept. Guy and the rest of the men changed, still in the same good spirits they had had on the coach. Guy began to focus his mind and psych himself up for what was ahead. He tried to leave any doubts raised by the importance and challenge of the match behind him and concentrate on what he knew he and his team-mates could do. He thought of how well they had played in the past couple of matches, how they were gelling more now that he was more accepted and after the progress they had made in practice. Once more, his thoughts turned to how his and Kyle's playing had improved after their special training sessions, deep down convinced that it could only get better now that another team-mate was involved.

After the men had changed, Lambert took centre stage, standing next to a whiteboard on the wall in front of the benches. The men quietened to pay attention to his run-through of the tactics and moves that had been planned for the game. It was merely a reminder of what had been discussed and worked on earlier in the week, but it gave Guy that extra conviction in what would be needed of him. The strategies were simple, but cleverly thought-out, attempting to defend Welby from Hadcastle's strengths, while attacking them at their weak points. Many of Welby's players had faced Hadcastle before and parts of Lambert's talk referred back to a previous game to highlight what he was saying. He mentioned the names of some of Hadcastle's men, taking care to explain to Guy what their gameplay was like. One name, Macca Brooks, was mentioned a few times. Brooks was a "good fellah, but a nasty player" Lambert told Guy, and was one who Guy should look out for in particular, as Lambert was sure he'd be marking him out, not only because the position he played meant he was an important link in pushing the team forward, but also because he'd be a new face to Brooks, and a southern, ex-Union player on top of that. Guy made a joke about the situation, thanking Lambert for the warning. He guessed there would be some extra work needed from him, but as unfriendly attitudes generated by his past were exactly what he had faced on his arrival at Welby, if he had dealt with them then, he was more than capable of dealing with them now.

"It'll be a tough match," Lambert told the team as he summarised. "Hadcastle haven't got where they are now for no reason. But neither have we. We're more than capable of meeting the best they can give us. And we've got plenty of reason today. We win this game and it's one step nearer to having that Cup in our hands. Just keep it tight, boys, play like a team and we'll be there."

Lambert gave a quick nod and a smile as he always did at the end of his pep talks. The men clapped, and a couple of them gave encouraging shouts as the team stood up and readied themselves for the walk out onto the pitch.

Moments later they were outside, listening to the roar of the crowd. Guy felt the now-familiar rush of excitement at the noise and the trepidation of the final few seconds before the match began. He examined his opponents carefully. They looked a formidable side of largely-built and fit men who seemed to show few nerves as they faced their opponents. Guy checked for the man he had been warned against, Macca Brooks, and found him in the line-up. He was a chunky fellow, around six-foot-tall with a definite bouncer-ish quality about him. He had a shaved head and a square-shaped face with small, but not unattractive features that were focused and intense, giving him an air of a man made for the rough and tumble of rugby. He stood with a physical confidence, hands behind his back so that his broad shoulders and chest stood out with pride. Guy saw no chinks in the man's armour of appearance and, deciding that what he had been told about him was true, made a mental note to keep an eye out for him.

Then the game began. Welby took early possession, but faced a ferocious attack from a seemingly relentless Hadcastle and lost the first points to them. The team didn't become disheartened, however, and struggled valiantly. Guy was surprised at just how good Hadcastle were and pushed himself to his limits both mentally and physically to help keep his team moving forward. It seemed as if, every time he got his hands on the ball, he faced a grimacing Macca Brooks, ready to launch himself at him. A couple of times, Brooks brought him down hard and Guy was shocked at how fierce and strong the man was. He knew he was being picked on but, not being one to let up in the face of a bully, he tried to avoid the man's tackles and often succeeded in getting the ball out of the way so that Welby could progress. The first half was a real fight and Guy could feel how stretched his team were. At the same time, he felt that the teams were evenly matched and sensed that victory was well within Welby's grasp. As the half-time whistle blew, they were behind, but not far behind, and as they faced Lambert once more, the conversation was encouraging.

"Well done, lads, you're playing well. We might be behind, but it's nothing we can't overcome if we carry on as we have been doing. It's an exciting match, there's some excellent gameplay, but you've just got to remember, keep hitting those weak points."

Lambert was forceful, not critical but direct and heartening and Guy felt revitalised by what the man was saying. He knew deep down that, as Lambert was trying to put across, it wasn't anybody's game yet and could be theirs. Despite Hadcastle's strengths, it was fully within Welby's capabilities to bring off a win. Going back out onto the pitch, Guy felt a new potency within him, which was bolstered by the opening minutes of the second half, which saw Welby gain some good ground as they faced Hadcastle once more with plays set up by Guy, Kyle and Mason. And then it was there again, the feeling Guy had sensed in the last match and on the coach on the way to Hadcastle. There was a link between him and the two team-mates he had had sex with, a new, intimate knowledge of each other's bodies, how they moved and worked, to the point where it seemed to Guy that each man knew what the other would do next, where they would be on the field and what move should be made to follow them up. It was as if they were parts of a machine, cogs fitting together to drive forward a great engine. It was an extremely powerful sensation and Guy felt sure that Kyle and Mason must be feeling it as well as they brought Welby to one try after another.

It still wasn't an easy game. Hadcastle fought impressively and were far from being completely overwhelmed. Macca Brooks kept up his onslaught on Guy, but against a man with such formidable back-up, Brooks' fury was simply not enough. Welby won the game with a good lead and, as Guy returned to the changing rooms, the ecstatic cheers of the Welby fans ringing in his ears, he felt elated that he and his team-mates had faced up to and met the challenge of tough, skilled opponents.

Lambert was similarly impressed with his team, and grinned broadly as he patted the backs of the players and congratulated them one by one.

"You did well out there today," Lambert told Guy. Then, in a loud voice so that the rest of the team could hear, he continued,

"Whatever's going on between you and Kyle seems to be spreading. It looks like you've got Mason involved now as well. But that's what I like to see, boys. Teamwork. Not just plays on your own, going for your own individual glory, players coming together to work as one."

The men began to change. As they stripped off for the shower, Lambert revealed he had a little surprise for them.

"You've been working hard lately and today has shown that the effort you've all put in has paid off." He shouted over the energised conversation of the Welby players. "I think you deserve a reward."

The team cheered at the good news.

"So I've booked a table for us all, and any of the Hadcastle players who can stand us, at a good, posh..."

"You'll feel at home then, Guy!" Mason interrupted, getting a laugh from all around.

"... restaurant in town."

The men made appreciative noises to show their gratitude.

"I know you boys might want to have a drink afterwards and I'm sure the Hadcastle fellahs will be happy to show you around some of the watering holes around town, so I've booked some local hotel rooms so you don't have to worry about getting back home tonight."

Now it was the men's turn to thank Lambert.

"Just what I needed," Kyle told his boss. "A good night out with the lads!"

"I'll tell you all now, rather than later when you've all had a drink," Lambert became fatherly. "Be careful. I know what some of you can be like when the booze is flowing and I know what some of the Hadcastle lads can be like. High jinks are allowed tonight, as long as they aren't too high, if you know what I mean. I don't want to be bailing you out of any police cells tomorrow morning, or waking up to some nasty headlines on Monday. Do you understand what I'm saying?"

The men groaned, like teenagers getting orders from their parents.

Guy felt excited. He and his team-mates did deserve a bit of a blow-out. It would be the first time they had done anything socially in a big group like that and he looked forward to interacting with his co-players in a situation that wasn't so focused on just the game.

Eleven

The men showered in good spirits, then dressed and prepared themselves for the night out. The coach that had brought them to Hadcastle drove them to the hotel in town that Lambert had booked so they could drop off their bags. From there, taxis were arranged to drive them to the restaurant. Hadcastle was a town known for its curry houses and Lambert had chosen one of the more respected ones. It was relatively small and its interior didn't compare in terms of expense to some of the restaurants Guy was used to in London, but there was a cosiness and friendliness to the place that he found very appealing. In addition, after such a tough match, he was ravenous and much more interested in what would be served than where he would be eating it.

"This'll hit the spot, right, fellahs?" Guy said as they entered the restaurant.

"A pint won't go amiss, either," Mason added, accidently bumping into a large man in a suit as he walked past the small bar in the entranceway. Mason apologised immediately, but it was too late. The man spun around quickly as if shocked or offended. To Guy's surprise and slight disappointment, the man turned out to be the Hadcastle player who had caused him the most trouble earlier in the day.

"I might have known," Brooks started. He raised himself up from his leaning position on the bar, puffing his chest out proudly and began nodding his head with not a little self-satisfaction. "The Welby boys. Can't keep the bodily contact on the pitch, eh, Mason?"

Sensing an abrupt end to the evening, Guy edged in to try to calm the situation.

"Come on, Brooks. It was just an accident," Guy put his hand on Brooks" left shoulder and attempted to wedge himself in between the man and Mason. "Now, what're you drinking?"

"Oh, it's the new boy, is it?" Brooks suddenly switched his attentions to Guy. "I wanted a word with you after what happened this afternoon. You know, when I knock somebody down they tend to stay down. You've got the nasty habit of getting up again. And again. And again."

Guy shrugged, attempting to look nonplussed, but at the same time not wanting to aggravate Brooks any further. "It's all in the way I fall," he said, nonchalantly.

Brooks stepped forward so that he was mere inches away from Guy and Guy could feel the man's breath on his cheeks. "Well, do you know what it means when that happens, new boy?"

Guy was beginning to lose his patience. He shook his head slightly, thinking of how he could alleviate the tension.

"It means you're a bloody good player, that's what!" Brooks' face broke into a huge, spontaneous smile. He grabbed hold of Guy's face and gave him a quick, comical kiss on the lips, before wrapping his arm around his neck and rubbing his head with his knuckles. The men around them burst into laughter. "Had you going for a minute then, Holbook, didn't I?"

Guy couldn't help but laugh along with them, partly out of relief at his dissipating apprehensions. A phrase that Lambert had used in describing Brooks suddenly came to his mind. Lambert had called Brooks a "good fellah but a nasty player". Guy surmised that he was now encountering the player's other side and was more than glad to after the beating he had taken on the pitch.

They were shown to their sizeable table and the men settled down to eat. There were quite a number of Hadcastle players, too, who had already arrived. Guy found himself seated near Brooks and as the meal (and the drinking) went on, he discovered him to be a incredibly likeable man. Without a doubt, he was a clown, a man who liked playing up to others, but the jokey side of his character was put on more to entertain than to get attention. His humour drew people in and often the table was silent to hear what he would say, before bursting into laughter at the quick, funny lines he came out with. He was the sort of man that other men love being around, who can put them at ease and cheer them with just a few well-placed words. During the early part of the evening, he worked to ease the relations between the two teams, so that the fact that they had opposed each other earlier on in the day was all but forgotten. Guy also began to find Brooks rather attractive. Brooks seemed totally at ease with himself and was manly and confident without being overbearing. He grinned often. It was infectious and Guy couldn't help but smile back at him, while enjoying his changing face, now masculine, now rough, now boyish.

It was Brooks who suggested the first port of call after the men had left the curry house, taking them to a reasonably busy local pub within walking distance. All had drunk with the meal, but were definitely ready for more and after a couple more pints, were laughing together and playing drinking games like old buddies at a reunion. Guy felt himself relaxing as he became gradually more drunk and it felt very good to cut loose. He took a lot of flak from both his own team and Hadcastle for not being from the North and being an ex-Union player, but all the ribbing was meant in fun and he often managed to dish out as many good-natured insults as he received. In fact, Guy really enjoyed it when anyone made a mock-critical comment about him. It showed how relaxed people felt in his presence now and how their relationships had developed so that they could take the mickey out of each other and not endanger the bonds that had grown.

A couple of pubs later, and the men became more raucous. They were thrown out of one bar for getting too involved in singing a particularly rude rugby song that required them dropping their trousers for the chorus. Although Guy had seen his team naked in the showers many times, the fact that he got to view the bums and cocks of his new Hadcastle friends was a source of great gratification to him. He couldn't help but pay particular attention to Brooks as he undid his trousers to reveal his chunky, but firm arse and a nicely sized, hairy packet that dangled and danced appealingly as Brooks waved his hips from side to side. He was very disappointed at the song's abrupt end and could only hope for a reprise as they entered another bar.

Another round of drinks was quickly ordered. The men were a little more subdued in their new surroundings, but Guy guessed it was just a result of them settling into a new pub. Only Brooks seemed to be continuing on in the same vein as before. He appeared to be slightly more drunk than the others, his voice carrying above the noise of the crowd and the music in the bar, his words slurring and his laughter raucous. Fortunately, he was in a good mood and it remained so even when an accident ended up with him pouring most of his drink over himself. He headed towards Guy, his smile as big as ever.

"Made a bit of a mistake," he mumbled, giggling, pointing to his wet shirt. "Better pay a visit to the little boys' room."

He squeezed past and, as he did so, gave Guy's backside a playful pinch. Surprised, Guy turned to see Brooks winking at him over his shoulder before disappearing into the toilet.

Guy shook his head, glad that he hadn't reached Brooks' state of drunkenness. He wondered whether there was anything else in Brooks' mischievous actions, but then dismissed his thoughts, deciding that his new friend was merely mucking around.

A couple of minutes later, a loud chanting made Guy turn. Behind him, the crowd of locals parted rapidly: Brooks hadn't simply stopped at rinsing his shirt off in the men's, but decided to completely strip off and was now wandering and singing through the bar wearing nothing but his boxer shorts on his head. The sight was partly funny, partly ridiculous and stupid, and more than a little arousing to Guy. It was the first time he had seen Brooks' body like that and it was a fine sight. Brooks was a chunky man, with a toned thickness to his limbs. Guy could see himself intertwined with him with no problem. He especially enjoyed the man's complete abandonment, his comfort with his body and at being naked around others and the way his dick bounced around to the movements of his silly dancing. A cheer of encouragement rose up from everyone in the bar, so he continued his entertainment. He moved up to Guy and in a mickey-take of a striptease, pouted his lips as he began to grind his hips in his direction. The move got a roar of laughter all around and, despite feeling rather embarrassed, Guy smiled, greatly appreciating the view. He was more than a little disappointed when Brooks spun round too quickly and lost his precarious balance. He fell, signalling the end of his impromptu show. Guy's compensation was that he could help him up, getting a good hold of the man's bare flesh as he did so.

"Holbrook," Brooks mumbled into Guy's ear as he held him up. "I think I might be a bit pissed. Give us a hand outside to get some fresh air."

"Well, let's get your pants on first, at least," Guy advised.

"But they're on me!" Brooks quipped, obviously not having lost his sense of humour along with his sense of balance.

Guy helped him step into his underwear, then wrapped the man's arm around his shoulder and helped him stumble out of the pub. There were groans of disappointment as they left from Brooks' the audience, sorry that the show was over.

Fortunately, the street outside was relatively quiet. Not wanting to attract attention, Guy led his friend down an alleyway at the side of the building and leant him against a wall so that he could calm down a little.

"Cheers, fellah," Brooks leant slightly against Guy. He seemed less wobbly and Guy guessed that the sudden burst of air had cleared his head.

"You know, I've been wanting to get you on your own all night," Brooks said, no longer slurring his words.

"Why's that, then?" Guy could see another punchline coming.

"Because I've been gagging to do this." Brooks straightened up, his actions steady, not at all those of someone who had had too much to drink. He inched closer, pausing just before his lips reached Guy's own, then leaned in and kissed him. Guy felt shocked, but more than ready to reciprocate, and within seconds, the two men's bodies were locked in a full-on embrace. The sensation of having a naked, well-built man so close was fantastic. Guy slid his hands down Brooks' back to where his underwear lightly covered his big, tight buttocks and took pleasurable, hearty squeezes of them. He could feel his own crotch thicken with excitement as Brooks' tongue invaded and explored his mouth. Likewise, he could feel Brooks' barely constricted length press hard against him, and he began rubbing his hips back and forth to pleasure the both of them.

Brooks pulled away slightly and the two men gave each other brief pecks, unable to keep their mouths distant for too long.

"I've seen you looking at me all night," Brooks said. He wasn't drunk at all now and Guy wondered if the strip and the inebriated act in the bar hadn't simply been a ploy to get him outside.

"Specifically at this." Brooks moved his body back and looked downwards. His boxer shorts pointed out at the front where his cock filled them. The shape was tantalisingly touchable and it twitched slightly as Brooks spoke once more. "I bet you'd love a bit of it."

"Oh, mate," Guy sighed. "Of course I fucking would." And then, wondering just how he'd ended up in this situation, he asked, "But how did you know I'd be interested?"

Brooks laughed briefly. "Word gets round, fellah. Not many secrets in the world of Rugby League, I can tell you. Anyway, that doesn't matter much now. We don't have much time here."

"Here?" asked Guy, nodding towards the end of the alley. The passageway was relatively dark, but the two men could see each other clearly, being illuminated by the light of a window above them. Guy couldn't see or hear anybody nearby, but the thought of being caught concerned him.

"Don't worry about that," Brooks reassured him. "Who's gonna bother two big lads like us? Now, there's something I want to know about you."

"What's that?" Guy was partly, but not fully at ease with their situation, but horny as he was, he decided he couldn't pass up the offer of an equally randy Brooks.

"Are your moves as good off the pitch as on it?" Brooks took up the cocksure, almost aggressive posturing he'd displayed in the restaurant earlier that evening.

Guy dropped to his knees. He slipped his fingers into the hemline of Brooks' boxer shorts, then eased it outwards and over the man's prick. Revealed, the thing was the same pale colour as the rest of his body. It was of an appealing, but not overwhelming thickness that tapered off to the end. Good and veiny, its foreskin ran right up to the tip where a circle of deep-pink glans peeped out, just begging to be licked.

"I don't know," Guy answered. "Tell me afterwards."

Guy took Brooks in his mouth, causing his friend to let out a hum of pleasure. Guy wiggled his tongue against the underside of the prick, sucked a couple of times, then moved himself down it. The muscle filled his mouth tantalisingly and he put his hands between his own legs to give his dick a quick rub through the material of his trousers. He began sliding up and down Brooks' pole, slowly and carefully and then, relaxing his gullet, he pushed himself completely on it so that it filled him nicely.

"Oh, mate," Brooks murmured above him. "Now that's deep fielding – that really hits the spot."

He placed a hand on Guy's head, not to force or keep him there, but to stroke him gently, as if to mirror exactly what was going on at his crotch. Guy mouthed the prick, wanting to give Brooks as good a time receiving the blowjob as he was having in giving it. He withdrew himself from it, but kept his open mouth right at the top, sticking his tongue out so that Brooks' bell end rested on it. He looked up at Brooks, finding him with his eyes half-shut and a dreamy, ecstatic expression on his face.

"Thank fuck for mouths like yours," Brooks complimented. "Good feed-in work, fellah. Really good work."

He took hold of his penis at the base and waggled it against Guy's tongue and lips so that they slapped together with little wet taps. Guy lunged for the thing, but Brooks pulled it away teasingly.

"Now, how's about we see how you are on ball control," Brooks said as he widened his legs. Guy shuffled himself downwards, eased his head between Brooks' thighs and began licking away. Brooks' bollocks were hairy and hung loose. Guy tasted the skin at side of them, rasping his tongue up and against the crack between Brooks' legs. Wanting the taste and sensation of another man's genitals in his mouth, it wasn't long before he was licking at Brooks' testicles properly, taking them inside and rolling them around the inside of his cheeks with his tongue. As he did so, Brooks began wanking himself off so that the saggy skin of his balls jiggled against Guy. Nuzzling further inwards, Guy let the saliva-dampened nuts rest against his face so that he could get his eager mouth further behind them. The strong, firm section of skin that led to Brooks' back passage was equally as hirsute as his balls. His smell and taste were strong there, reeking of beautiful hormone-filled sweat. It was a very sensitive place – as Guy explored it, Brooks moaned louder, and swore a couple of times to egg his fuck-buddy on. Instinctually, Guy guessed what Brooks really wanted and stopped his sucking.

"Turn around, big fellah," he advised. "I want to see you from your best angle."

Brooks did as he was told, muttering a good-humoured "cheeky fucker" as he did so. He bent over, then reached behind himself to take hold of his buttocks, splaying them so that Guy could see right up his crack.

"How's that?" asked Brooks.

Guy took in the view. Brooks' bumcheeks were hairless, but inside, following up and around from between his legs was a smattering of pubes that circled his anus delightfully. His sphincter looked good and tight, a wrinkled star that trembled, then puckered at its owner's excitement.

"Good goal sighting," Guy praised. "How's this for tight play?"

He stuck his tongue out as far as it would go, then shoved his face right in between Brooks' spread arse. He tickled the exposed ringpiece with the tip of his outstretched tongue, wiggling around it, then taking a couple of good solid licks. The skin was taut but yielding and it had the feel of no other place on a man's body. The taste was exquisite, a musky and forbidden mixture of secret body odours. He shoved his tongue in and the man's crevice gripped him as he fought against the tightness of the muscles. Brooks groaned at the insertion and, to add to his pleasure, Guy reached in between his legs, gripping first his balls and giving them a squeeze, then working his hand along Brooks' stiff shaft to give it a good wank.

"Penetrate the field, mate," Brooks encouraged, as his prick oozed a little pre-come over Guy's fingers. Guy did as he was told, increasing the ferocity of his explorations so that his tongue was up Brooks as far as it would go. Guy began making short jerky movements with his neck, fucking Brooks' arse. And then, guessing Brooks was ready for something more up there, he spat on his middle finger, then slowly slipped it up his friend. Brooks shuddered and groaned as Guy frigged him, simultaneously kissing and licking around Brooks' anus and over his buttocks. Guy felt incredibly horny. Here he was, his finger and face up the arse of a big, burly, naked man in a place that, if not public, was far from private. The fact that they could get caught at any second in such a delicate situation scared him, but thrilled him even more and soon enough his thoughts turned to the further stimulation of his own cock.

"I've got to go deep, Brooks," Guy said, as he steadily drove a second finger home. "You've got a beautiful arse. I've got to put it up."

It was true enough. Brooks' backside was beautiful. Big, round and inviting, it stayed firm against every kiss and caress and its entrance promised future delights aplenty.

"Give it your best shot," Brooks said. "I'm ready to receive."

Guy stood up. He took a condom and a packet of lube out of his wallet, then undid his belt. His dick, up to that moment having been comparatively left out of the action, was rock hard, desperate for physical contact. He released it from his underwear, dropping them and his trousers around his ankles. The cool night air tickled his skin as he rubbered up, but he barely registered the cold, being too excited by what was happening. Guy ripped open the lube and squirted some out, first onto Brooks' behind, and then onto his own erection. He squirmed his fingers back up Brooks to fully grease the man, at the same time coating himself with the lube with his other hand. And then, both men more than ready for the insertion, Guy shuffled forward, directing his steely rod towards the dark, pouting target in front of him. Steadily and firmly, he pushed his hips and tool forward so that Brooks' hole had no choice but to accept him. And accept him it did, opening up slowly to envelop him with an unyielding grasp. Soon enough, Guy was up there to the hilt, both men completely joined together in physical joy. Guy let himself rest there for a few seconds, just enjoying the wonderful grip of Brooks upon him. He wrapped his arms around Brooks' naked torso, copping a good feel of his thick chest, playing with his raised nipples, then running his hands over his filled, toned belly. He moved back slightly, placed his hands either side of Brooks' waist and gave his first shunt.

"That's the stuff, fellah," moaned Brooks. "That's bloody lovely."

Guy followed the action up with a second, then a third buck and soon built up a steady and sure rhythm. The squelching noises of him entering and vacating Brooks, coupled with both the men's murmurs and groans, provided a dirty, echoing soundtrack to their lovemaking.

"Force it, Guy, push it," Brooks urged his chum. "I can take it."

More than happy to oblige, Guy gave him a sudden, hard fuck, dragging the man onto him. Brooks' wincing "yes" indicated that the move was well appreciated and so Guy did it again, stepping up the pace to buffet his friend's behind, the shags penetrating him good and deep. The movements and added stimulation took Guy's excitement up a notch and he could feel himself getting closer and closer to orgasm. He reached around Brooks' waist and took hold of the man's prick once more. It was very sticky now and it jumped in his hand at his touch. Guy decided he wanted to bring Brooks' off first, wanting to feel the man ejaculate in his hands, his arse squeezing around his cock, so he began to wank him off.

"I'm close," Brooks warned. "Are you ready for a palm-off?"

"Yes." Guy barely had the time to fuck Brooks again before the man in his arms grunted like a wild beast, then began to shake violently. Guy felt the prick in his grasp stiffen to an unbelievable hardness, then jerk as it shot its first load of spunk. His fingers became coated with hot jism, bringing him to higher states of ecstasy, as Brooks' rectum spasmed, grasping, relaxing and regrasping his dick as if trying to milk his spunk out of his last few fucks. Guy could hold back no longer. The situation was simply too arousing for him and he let himself go at last. Pleasure took hold of his body and mind completely, growing from a mere tingling sensation in his belly and at the end of his dick and then spreading to possess him entirely as his muscles stiffened to a point of near tension, then relaxed into wave upon wave of repeated joy. His prick jolted as it let loose round after round of spunk within Brooks and he could feel the heat as his own liquid coated his love-muscle within the condom and Brooks' back passage continued to undulate around him. Gradually, a warm calm settled on him as the throbs of his penis lessened and he let himself rest on Brook's hefty back, not wanting to exit his friend until his body had finally finished its journey into bliss. Eventually, he withdrew himself, and Brooks turned around to give him a grateful kiss. Brooks felt good in his arms after the orgasm, like a full stop to complete the sentence of the sexual act.

"So what do you think, Brooks?" Guy asked his friend as they settled into the clinch. "Have I made the team?"

Brooks looked puzzled, then his face broke into a smile.

"Definitely," he said, dreamily. "You can be my Man of the Match any day!"

Guy laughed, then kissed him once more. "Do you think you will have 'recovered' enough to go back inside?"

"Yeah," Brooks shrugged. "Could do with a 'post-match' pint."

"Let's go for it, then." Guy was having a great night, and the thought of continuing the evening's proceedings with the rest of his friends in the bar was very appealing. He and Brooks began cleaning themselves up. Guy pulled off the condom carefully and wiped himself and his hands down with a handkerchief. "Don't get too drunk, though," he warned his buddy.

"Why's that?" Brooks asked.

"I fancy a replay later," he winked, giving him a playful spank on the behind as they walked off towards the bar.

Twelve

Guy and Brooks had not actually been gone that long and Guy found himself returning just in time to put his order in for a round bought by Mason. A couple of the men inquired after Brooks and Guy told them that he thought he was feeling a lot better. Sure enough, as if to prove the point, Brooks emerged from the toilets where he had left his clothes, ready to dish out his individual brand of humour again. He received a cheer, which he accepted gratefully, along with another pint of bitter, slipping a sly, knowing look across at Guy, and thanking him profusely for his "help". In terms of boozing, the night didn't last that much longer for either Guy or Brooks. They followed their friends to a local club but, finding themselves much more interested in each other than dancing, drinking or pulling the women there, they slipped away from the rest of the group after the first hour to the hotel that had been booked for the Welby players. They made love repeatedly, enjoying each other's bodies and company greatly, sleeping briefly before waking up to fuck again.

Guy got out of bed properly just before midday. Fortunately, having predicted the state the team would be in after their night out, Lambert had booked the hotel for two days, allowing for delayed rising. Guy felt, despite a slight hangover, pretty damn good. His team had won a hard game, he had had a great night out and he'd screwed a sexy beast of a man who still lay sleeping in his bed.

He showered, the water washing off the worst of his bad head so that he felt good about the rest of the day. He considered his options, deciding that what he really fancied doing was taking it easy, spending some time on his own, perhaps later even taking a drive into the nearby countryside. He dressed, as Brooks finally awoke. The two men chatted for a while, Brooks trying to persuade Guy to come back to bed. Guy was tempted, but knew if he didn't leave then he would probably still be there that evening, or even later. With training in the morning, that would not be the best of plans. But he liked Brooks a lot and, although he knew there would be nothing for them in terms of a romantic relationship, he hoped that further friendly and sexual encounters would be on the cards. The two men were relaxed in each other's company and definitely attracted to each other, and they exchanged phone numbers before Guy left, promising to meet up again once more.

Guy had a quick breakfast in the hotel's restaurant, before heading off to the train station to catch a train back to Welby. He was back at his flat before 2.00pm and was waving his fob in front of the magnetic lock to the front entrance door when a voice behind him stopped him.

"Hello, stranger!" The voice was instantly recognisable. Guy turned to find its owner, who almost leapt at him to give him a big hug and a kiss.

"H-Hugo!" Guy exclaimed, gobsmacked. "What are you doing here?"

"I've come to rescue you," Hugo began. "From this drab world of grim buildings and in-bred locals!"

"How did you know I'd be here?" Guy felt a little shaken.

"I saw your car outside. I guessed you'd not gone far. I'm parked just across the road so I waited there for you to come back. It's only taken an hour or so."

Guy saw his relaxing afternoon alone melt away in front of his eyes. At that moment, Hugo, dominating and demanding, was one of the last people he wanted to see.

"Where've you been, anyway? One-night stand?" Hugo was joking, but little did he know he'd hit the nail more or less on the head.

"Er... me and the boys had a night out after the match. Stayed in a hotel in Hadcastle."

"Hadcastle? I drove through that dump on the way here." Hugo rolled his eyes to emphasise his horror. "Must have been a thrilling night."

"If only you knew," Guy thought to himself.

"And listen to you," Hugo continued, lighting up a cigarette. "'Me and the boys...' Anybody would think you liked it up here."

"I do," Guy snapped. He had begun to feel weary of Hugo already.

Hugo pulled a silly-looking "oops!" face. "Well, are you going to invite me in or shall we just carry on our conversation out here?"

Guy half-wanted to tell him to come back later. What he really fancied doing was getting his feet up on the sofa and relaxing in front of some old movie on the TV rather than play frustrating mind games with Hugo. But he guessed Hugo meant well: the man had made a surprise trip, and was probably sensing something amiss at Guy's lack of enthusiasm. He decided to put some more effort into it.

"Come on, then," he said as he finally opened the door. "We've got some catching up to do."

Upstairs, Guy busied himself making coffee while Hugo looked around the flat. Hugo was actually quite complimentary about the place, liking the design and what Guy had done with it, but he couldn't stop himself from expressing surprise that Welby would have anything so new on offer and dissing the location. Afterwards, he turned the conversation to his favourite topic – himself – and began regaling Guy with tales of friends and foes from London, what parties he had been to, who was seeing or sleeping with whom, who was up and who was down. Guy had never really been part of Hugo's social scene, merely hanging around on the outskirts by default. A lot of the people Hugo was talking about he barely knew and a lot of them he had never liked anyway. So the conversation, in which he seemed only to be playing a cursory role, struck him as dull and pretty vacuous. He began to wonder whether Hugo had always been like that, or whether he was finding Hugo that way because he was slightly tired from the night before and wound up by Hugo's comments about Welby and his new life.

"So, you *can* get decent coffee up here!" Hugo laughed, as he took a sip from the cup Guy handed him. "I stopped off in town earlier to see if there was anywhere I could get a fix of caffeine. I really felt like an espresso, or something. As you know, there's nowhere. I ended up in a greasy café, drinking a mug of tea with too much milk in it. It was a disgusting place!"

"Betty's." Guy guessed where Hugo meant. He sat down on the sofa near, but not too near, his friend. "I like it there. They do a mean fry-up. And it's only £2."

Hugo began to laugh, but stopped when he realised Guy was not joking.

"I'm glad you've settled in so well," he said, unconvincingly. "This kind of culture suits some people better than others."

"Obviously," Guy snapped. Hugo looked contrite.

"Oh, don't let's argue, darling. I'm only here for a few days, and most of that time I'm going to be working. We might as well enjoy what time we have got together. I thought we'd have a lovely evening tonight. We could go back to my hotel, order champers from Room Service…"

"You're working?" Guy was surprised. Hugo flitted from meaningless job to meaningless job, relying on his family's riches to subsidise him every time he got the sack, or merely couldn't be bothered to go in any more. He had never before been employed in a position that involved having to travel.

"Yes, unfortunately. Daddy thought it was time I did something useful for a change. He's become rather tight on the purse strings of late. I had to start working for him to make sure I kept hold of at least some of my allowance."

Guy found himself smirking. Hugo in a proper job? Working for his father? It was something that would either make or break the young man, as Guy supposed Hugo's parents must have decided themselves.

"So, what are you doing? I didn't even know your father had any business up here?"

"Oh, it's nothing major. Some company he owns up here. He selling it off and I'm here to help out with the closure of one of the factories. To tell you the truth, I don't really know much about it. I couldn't be bothered to read the brief."

"It's Cooper's Mill, isn't it?" Guy asked, as realisation dawned.

"That's right. Bloody ugly building, from the looks of it. I bet the locals will be glad to see it go."

Guy was incensed. The man simply had no idea what he had become part of.

"Glad to see it go?" Guy's voice rose in fury. "That factory supports livelihoods here. It supports families and communities. It supports the town, Hugo. If that place goes, then for a lot of people, so does Welby."

"My God," Hugo looked mildly amused by Guy's outburst. "I was wrong about you. You haven't just settled in here, someone's taken over your body and made you obsessed with the place."

He took a particularly long drag on his cigarette before continuing. "Don't you realise it's the North of England? Unemployment is *supposed* to happen here."

Guy boiled at Hugo's insensitivity and coldness. "Those are my friends you're talking about," he shouted. "They've taken me in like a family member since I showed them what I could achieve here. They're my people now. They're my…"

"Lovers?" Hugo interrupted with a raised eyebrow.

Guy closed his eyes and shook his head. He just couldn't believe what Hugo was doing, how he had become involved in the closure of the factory. He was so livid, he felt completely unable to deal with the man. He would rather never have to deal with him again.

"Hugo, I think you'd better leave," he said, walking over to his front door.

"But, darling, what about tonight?" Despite Guy's anger, he didn't care that he'd overstepped the mark.

"Surprisingly, I've lost interest." Guy paused and reached a conclusion that had been imminent for a long while. "Actually, Hugo, I've lost interest in any future 'tonights'."

Hugo tutted. He shrugged, stood up, then walked disdainfully towards the door.

"Well, just don't come crawling back to me when he, whoever he is, loses interest in your middle-class accent!" he sneered as he left.

"Bye, Hugo," Guy said to his receding back, but received no reply.

Deep down, Guy had known for a long time that their relationship was over. He had not wanted it to end that way, with animosity between them. However, he had felt so irritated by Hugo's constant swipes about his new home and then so flabbergasted by his lack of awareness about the consequences of his actions, that he had become too enraged not to lash out. He swore as he shut the door, frustrated with himself but more so with his now ex-boyfriend for making him feel that way. He collapsed backwards onto his settee, trying to console himself with the notion that maybe one day he and Hugo would be friends. At the moment – *definitely* at the moment – they were much better off not being part of each other's lives. He turned on the TV to distract himself, realising the irony in the fact that he had got the afternoon alone he wanted after all and yet wasn't going to be enjoying it at all.

Thirteen

The following few weeks were hard work for Guy. He continued to put in his hard work at Welby and he and his team continued to improve. Their performance wasn't perfect and they did lose or draw a match here and there, but it was still very good. Guy always felt he and his team-mates could hold their heads up high when they ran out onto the pitch, or were spotted in the street. He really believed that Welby's matches provided something for people to look forward to at the weekend and their excellence gave them something to be proud of in a time that wasn't good. He truly felt accepted into the town. Apart from the sole exception of Georgie Grant, whose displeasure at Guy's presence had diminished to a mere occasional jibe, he felt fully integrated into his team. His closeness with his team-mates continued to grow. Guy knew this was partly due to the increased length of time they had spent together, which had now grown into months, and partly due to the special training sessions.

As he had promised, Gripper Mason did manage to "recruit" a couple of the other Welby players for some close contact work after Reeves had finished with the team – two men who were greatly interested in and happy to take part in the sessions. Five-men sessions were regularly organised and soon became six as a further team member came across the group one day, much as Mason had done earlier in the season. Their physical intimacy once more promoted their skills on the pitch and Welby played as a tightly focused unit. The progress was noticed by Lambert and

Reeves at the club, as well as outsiders, the sports press and the fans themselves. The word was that this was the best side Welby had had in years and no little praise went Guy's way for providing the catalyst. Guy felt great about what had happened at Welby and how all his hard work and efforts both on the pitch and off it had paid off.

He didn't feel so good about what was happening with the strike, however. Ever since his row with Hugo, he had worried about the futility of his and the strike team's efforts. He guessed that, if Hugo was involved, all the important negotiations of the deal must already be over and all that was left was a tidying-up process. He stayed away from the factory for the first week after he had seen Hugo, hoping that he could avoid seeing him again. But there were a couple of times in the weeks afterwards when Guy saw him driving into or out of the car park at Cooper's Mill. No contact was made between them. Guy didn't even know if he had been spotted by Hugo and thought that Hugo would probably be rather surprised if he did. The experience made him feel incredibly awkward, as if in some bizarre way he was tied up in the wrong side of the fight against the closure. He began to feel like he was holding back information from the strikers and, though he continued to turn up along with some of the other players every few days after training, he felt there was something that prevented him from giving as much to the cause as he had previously. His efforts were undercut by a sense of sadness. He found it hard to develop his relationship with Shaw and the progress the two of them had made so far stopped. There was a distance between them that Guy just couldn't overcome, despite his genuine and serious feelings for the man. He knew that, once the strike was over, he would have little reason to see him, but also realised that any barrier he felt existed between them was one that only he could break down. He remained unsure of what move to make and so the trouble festered for quite a while.

Things came to a head one day. Guy had spent about an hour with the strikers and was on his way back to his car, feeling frustrated, when a heavy hand tapped him on the shoulder.

"I want a word with you."

Guy's heart sank even further. It was Nutter Harris, obviously up for more trouble. Guy wasn't in the mood.

"If this is about my patronising attitude, Harris..." he began, willing to risk the chance that he might end up with a black eye. To his surprise, Harris interrupted him calmly.

"No, it's not that. Not at all, Guy," Harris seemed a little unsure of himself. "I want to apologise. For the way I've acted towards you in the past."

Guy was shocked. He didn't know what to say, so simply let Harris continue.

"I was mistaken. I'd got the wrong impression of you. What you've done for the people here and for the team, has made me see you in a completely different light. You're a good 'un."

He grasped Guy by the shoulder. To Guy's further surprise, his face broke into a rather appealing smile.

"Sorry, mate," he beamed with humility.

"Well, I accept your apology." Guy felt suddenly cheered. It may not have seemed so, but his efforts did apparently mean something to some people. Never one to bear grudges, he decided that this would be a good opportunity for him and Harris to patch things up.

"How's about a drink to show there're no hard feelings?" he asked, his spirits lightened.

Harris was delighted with the idea. "I'd love one!" he grinned.

"There's a pub not too far from here, isn't there? I'll give you a lift if you want."

Harris looked slightly sheepish. "Oh... I'm off the booze for a while. I think I was letting it get on top of me. But how's about a cuppa at mine?"

"To tell you the truth," Guy confessed. "I think that would suit me even better than a pint right now!"

Harris lived in one of the older areas of Welby. Some of the streets on his estate were converted terraces and some streets looked rather dilapidated to Guy as he drove past them.

"It's this one on the corner here," Harris told Guy as they reached a small semi. "Park up on the drive, if you like."

Guy did so and the two men got out and entered the house.

"Like I said," Harris continued as he brought Guy his drink into the lounge. "I'd got the wrong end of the stick when I first met you. I was under Georgie's influence quite a bit. I've made up my own mind about you now."

Guy took a sip from his mug. "And what's your conclusion?" he asked.

Harris raised his eyebrows and looked squarely at Guy. His face was open and friendly in a way it had never been before. Guy found what he saw attractive and striking.

"Not bad," Harris winked. "Not bad at all."

For a second, Guy wondered whether Harris was flirting with him and then dismissed the thought.

"You and Grant good friends, then?" he asked, interested in getting more background information on both men.

"Yeah," Harris confirmed. "You could say we've been more than that, but we've been having some bad times lately. Lots of arguments and stuff. That's why I was hitting the bottle so hard, why he's been so bad-tempered all the time."

Guy was puzzled. Were Harris and Grant lovers? Realising he was in difficult territory, he decided to let the answer unfold, rather than attempt to prise it out.

"Think we need to spend some time apart for a while. Think we can have bad effects on each other sometimes," Harris continued.

The up-side of Harris and Grant's break from each other appeared to be working already. Sober and composed, Harris seemed a different man, hardly the 'Nutter' of old at all. The aggression that had been his key characteristic seemed to have been replaced by a solid, rolling comfort, as if his demons had finally been chased away. What had emerged was a down-to-earth, rough-around-the-edges angel, stable, big-built and handsome.

Distracted by his new impression of the man, Guy lost his grip on the mug of tea he was holding and it dropped completely from his hand. Fortunately, the liquid inside was not too hot, but it covered him from chest to lap.

"Shit!" He swore in surprise.

"Bloody hell, Guy!" Harris laughed at his error. "You never show butterfingers like that on the pitch. What's wrong with you?"

He stood up. "You couldn't have spread that any further if you'd tried. Come on upstairs. I must have something you can borrow to drive home in. I'll give your shirt a quick rinse under the tap while you're finding something."

Guy followed Harris upstairs into a room that was obviously Harris' bedroom. Harris disappeared for a couple of seconds, then returned with a towel in his hand.

"You're soaked. Take your shirt off. I'll find you something to replace it." Harris rummaged in his wardrobe, pulling out a T-shirt and some tracksuit bottoms.

"And the rest," he pointed to Guy's jeans which had also become rather drenched.

"It'll dry," Guy felt suddenly unsure of himself, and the situation.

"It'll stain, more like. No point in ruining a pair of jeans for no reason."

It had never occurred to Guy that Harris might have a 'happy homemaker' side to him, but here it was, unashamed and helpful. Perhaps too helpful.

Guy now stood naked apart from his socks and underwear. Harris moved over to him, picking up the towel once more.

"You can have a shower if you like," he said. He looked a little nervous.

"I'll be fine. It was only tea," Guy reassured him.

Harris smiled. His face looked benevolent and caring. Guy felt himself warming to him by the second.

"You're still wet," Harris pointed out. He gingerly raised the towel to Guy's chest and began dabbing at the damp patch on it. Guy's eyes met his and he looked away. It was the first time Guy had seen Harris anything but arrogant and it suited him, making him more appealing.

"Down here as well." Harris moved the towel to Guy's belly, giving it a good rub. The touch was not heavy-handed, as one might have expected from a man of his size and nature, but careful yet determined, like that of a knowledgeable lover. Feeling increasingly enchanted by the man and pretty sure by that point that he knew his intentions, Guy decided to make a risky move.

"Here." Guy took hold of Harris' hand and moved it downwards to his thighs where some of his drink had soaked through his jeans. To Guy's pleasure, Harris didn't flinch or hurry over the task, but rubbed Guy's thigh slowly and gently, gradually getting higher until the towel he held jiggled Guy's balls. Guy was immediately aroused and his penis thickened.

"Your pants are wet," Harris told Guy. "They'll have to come off, too."

"Okay," Guy agreed. He slipped out of his black briefs and threw them on the bed. He knew that his erection, though not full, would be noticeable and he thrilled inwardly at displaying himself to Harris.

Without speaking, Harris tenderly wiped over Guy's penis with the towel. Guy became even more aroused and his dick started to rise higher and higher to meet Harris' touch.

"Pretty sensitive man, eh?" asked Harris, looking downwards.

"Sorry," Guy shrugged. "Couldn't help it."

"You like showing yourself off like that, do you?" Harris asked. Guy nodded.

"Why don't you lie down and I'll take a good look at you," Harris continued. "I like to watch as much as you like to show off."

Guy lay back on the bed, his fully stiff prick falling back against his belly.

"Blimey! That's a lovely cock you've got," Harris shook his head from side to side in appreciation. He reached out and tugged on Guy's member a few times, rubbing at his own crotch with his other hand. "Feels good to touch, as well. Do you like that?"

Guy murmured "yes" as waves of pleasure began to wash over his body. Harris licked a finger, then wiped it on the underside of Guy's dick, tickling it up and down on its most sensitive section.

"Show us your arse, Guy. I bet you've got a beautiful hole," he said.

More than happy to oblige, Guy raised his legs so that his quads rested against his chest and stomach and his backside split to reveal its contents. He felt delightfully dirty showing himself off like that.

"I wasn't wrong there," Harris complimented. "That's lovely. Now how's about you finger yourself. I'd love to see something inside you."

Feeling increasingly excited, Guy quickly licked the middle finger of his left hand, then reaching downwards, slipped it inside himself. The insertion sent a thrill to his pleasure circuits that seemed even more intense than usual as a result of being watched. He frigged his rectum a few times, all the time watching Harris' reaction. Harris was grasping and squeezing at his own crotch, although he left his dick inside his jeans. He looked excited, and his chest rose and fell quickly with the increase in his breathing. He leaned over, pushing Guy's legs back further so that his arse rose higher in the air, giving Harris a better view. Harris' face screwed up with his excitement and he nodded at Guy as if to show his gratitude.

"I've got something better we could put up there if you like," he said

"What's that, then?" Guy asked, removing his finger.

"How about this?" Harris stuck his tongue out and wiggled it from side to side playfully.

"That'll do nicely," Guy murmured. Harris dived downwards. Guy felt the initial proddings of a couple of fingers, the warmth of Harris' breath up his split cheeks, then the wet, inquisitive tongue pressing against his ringpiece. He looked down through his splayed thighs to see Harris' forehead bumping against his balls as he nuzzled up the open crevice. Then Harris fully inserted his tongue, opening up Guy's back passage, causing Guy to let out a relief-filled moan of passion. Guy felt the thing exit, re-enter and exit him again, then lick around and around so that more and more of his arse became wet with spit. He felt incredibly horny and wanted more than anything to feel something sizeable inside him.

"Got anything else you could put up there?" he asked at last.

Harris raised himself once more. "I think I might have," he said fiddling with his fly. Without undoing his belt, he reached inside his jeans and pulled out his dick. "Will this do?" He took hold of the thing by the base and gave it a good waggle.

Guy lowered his legs again and reached for it. It was his turn now to have a good look. The dick was about seven inches in length, relatively thin and smooth-looking, with a circumcised head perfectly in proportion with the rest of it. Guy wanked him a few times, making the man wince with the first contact.

"It certainly will," Guy said giving Harris' nuts a frisky squeeze.

Harris rummaged briefly in the top drawer of a bedside cabinet, taking out a condom and a packet of lube. He lowered his jeans and underwear to his thighs, then quickly rubbered up as Guy lubricated himself. Harris took hold of Guy by the waist, then roughly dragged him in one swift movement to the edge of the bed. Guy swooned inwardly, feeling as if he was being taken by a real bloke, and was more than ready to submit. Harris knelt down, slipped one of Guy's legs over his shoulder, then began to poke around at Guy's arse with his prick. Before long, he had found the entrance and slowly but surely entered Guy. The insertion hurt, but was also, as always, intensely pleasurable.

"You all right, mate?" Harris asked, noticing Guy wince.

"Yeah," Guy reassured him. "Pretty damn good."

Harris smiled. "Well, I'm going to make you feel even better." He eased his hips back and then forward again. The first fuck was quickly but easily followed by another, then another until a steady, comfortable rhythm had been built up. Guy enjoyed the sensation of being pleasured by and pleasuring Harris. That his fuck-buddy was almost fully clothed was a further great source of arousal, feeling as he did enjoyably exposed and naked.

Harris shoved himself deep into Guy, then leaned over him so that their faces met.

"Shame I never realised the truth about you earlier," he said.

"Funny, that," Guy whispered in his ear. "I was thinking exactly the same thing."

The two men kissed, neither tentative nor reticent, but immediately passionate and forceful. They were both desperate for each other, Guy wrapping his arms around Harris and holding him as closely as he could manage. He slid an arm downwards to Harris' naked backside, taking a good pinch of it, then pulling it towards him so that Harris' dick was forced further up inside him. He tightened the muscles of his rectum to increase the sensation of being plugged up by man-meat like that.

"Oh, you want more, do you?" Harris asked, raising himself once more.

"Yes, please," Guy confirmed, ready to take a good pounding.

"Well, I'll just have to give it to you then, won't I?" Harris pulled himself almost fully out of Guy, then shunted back up him rapidly. He repeated the action and then got faster. Lying prone, there was little Guy could do to meet Harris' bucking. Instead, he could only lie back and enjoy being a fully willing receptacle for his friend. He began to wank himself off, watching as Harris' huge body slammed into him again and again, taking delight in the man's reddening, eager, determined face and the ease and confidence he displayed in fucking. If there was ever a man to be passive for, Guy thought, it was Nutter Harris, a big masculine beast who obviously loved and was well-practised in sex.

Guy reached up to feel Harris' large chest and well-formed belly as it pounded against the backs of his legs. Harris closed his eyes and stuck his tongue out of the corner of his mouth as if concentrating. He began to shag faster. Guy grabbed hold of his own ball sac with his other hand to bring himself off, basking in the utter glory of being shafted hard and fast by such a rough fucker. His dick grew even bigger and harder in his hand, his enjoyment increasing to a peak and centralising itself on the very tip of his cock. He jerked at himself with abandon, grimacing as he reached orgasm and his member spurted away, covering his torso and hand with hot, white fluid. He could feel his rectum spasm around Harris' prick, bringing him to even greater heights of ecstasy. He was lost in space and time. At the point where he couldn't take any more of the sheer bliss his body had to show him, the intensity decreased.

"Nearly there," Harris panted, fucking away hard at Guy. "Nearly..." He broke off what he was saying as his body became rigid. His face took on an expression of utter fulfilment and his shunts slowed right down into a set of steady, staccato, full in-out movements. Guy could feel the quivering of Harris' dick within him and thrilled at the thought of it shooting all that lovely man-milk inside his arse. Harris leaned over him, taking him in his arms as his body relaxed. He looked very, very happy. He kissed Guy once again, this time more gentle and affectionate, now that they had achieved satisfaction.

They looked at each other deeply, before Harris grinned.

"Not bad for a southerner," he joked rolling off to lie at Guy's side.

"Watch what you're saying!" Guy warned, ruffling his fingers through his new friend's hair. "Or I won't be letting you do that again!"

It was a long time before Guy felt like getting dressed. He lay comfortably with his head on Harris' chest, one of Harris' arms wrapped round him. Neither of them said much at first, both simply enjoying the calm after the storm of their lovemaking. Guy felt good about the sense of ease between them, that they didn't have to fill the silence with conversation, meaningless or otherwise. Then, as their energies returned, they began to ask each other questions, genuinely interested in what their lives had been like in the years previous to their meeting. Harris revealed a lot about himself, the troubles he'd had with his family and his father in particular, that he was trying to put behind him. He spoke more about his relationship with Georgie Grant. He was, if not positive for its future, at least positive for his own, whether it involved Grant or not. In turn, Guy felt open enough to talk about his life, speaking of, among other things, his recent split with Hugo. Eventually, the conversation turned to the strike, and specifically to the strike team's leader, Shaw Davies. Harris began to laugh.

"So, you like him as much as he does you?"

Guy was surprised, believing he had kept his feelings for Davies as hidden as he could.

"But I didn't say anything about..." he began.

"You didn't have to," Harris said. "It was obvious from the look in your eyes." Harris was obviously a lot sharper than his bruiser persona suggested.

"And you think he feels the same way?" Guy felt suddenly excited.

"Well, he talks about you enough when you're not around. Always singing your praises, and that. If he's not interested, he's got a funny way of showing it."

Guy's head reeled. He hoped that what Harris was saying was true. Maybe there were aspects of Shaw's behaviour that he just hadn't picked up on and he couldn't wait to see the man again to check out if Harris' suspicions were correct...

Guy left Harris after another cup of tea (which he drank this time) and a shower, returning to his flat to settle in for the evening. He had not been home long when the phone rang. It was his mother, checking in for her usual progress report on his life. As ever, she was pleased to hear about how well the team were doing and how much Guy was enjoying himself in Welby. She was disappointed, however, when she asked Guy about the strike. Guy couldn't hide his concerns over the future of the strikers, revealing to her for the first time his collision with Hugo a few weeks ago and what he had interpreted his presence in Welby to mean.

"I suppose you're right," she said, forlornly. "If that layabout is involved, the serious work must all be over and done with."

Her disdain for Hugo rose to the surface quite readily now that he was less of a feature in Guy's life.

"He's working for his father, you say?" she enquired. "Poor old David. I wonder if he knows what he's letting himself in for."

"Have you seen much of him recently?"

"No, and that's a shame really. We used to get on so well." She paused for a moment, and then continued in a much brighter tone of voice. "Maybe I should give them a call. They can't possibly have any real idea of the trouble the factory closure is causing. I could have a word with them, couldn't I, see if I could help in any way?"

Guy couldn't really see what his mother could do, but didn't see any harm in letting her get involved. "I don't see why not," he told her. "Although I don't hold out much hope."

"Oh, think positive, darling. You should never underestimate the power of an old friend in any situation. Leave it with me. I'll ring them straight after this."

They spoke for a few minutes more, then said their goodbyes. Guy began making his evening meal. He didn't really believe that his mother could do much. He knew there was a lot of money involved in the deal, and surely it was too far gone for anything to change now. Still, he liked the support and sympathy she was offering.

Fourteen

For the rest of that season, Welby played excellently, gradually working their way up to the top of the League table. Interest in them reached an all-time high, with media coverage extending past local and regional items to slots on national sports programmes and interviews for newspapers and magazines. Guy found himself contacted quite regularly by journalists for articles and ended up even providing copy for a couple of men's magazines. Although he wasn't the only Welby player to generate interest, Guy did find that he was one of the more popular ones. He put this down to being relatively new in the team and having a good tale to tell, having started his career at Welby as a fish out of water in more ways than one. The emphasis on the team and the opinion generally held by many was that the side was a classic line-up that had stand-out players combined with great teammanship. As such, Guy often found himself asked just exactly what was Welby's secret. He always held back on his answer, though, knowing how surprised people would be if they only knew the truth.

Having played so well, Welby deservedly found themselves in the Cup Final. In the week before the match, Reeves pushed the team as hard as ever during training. Though they had done admirably so far, the team that they would be opposing in the final were a strong side and they couldn't afford to become complacent.

Guy desperately wanted to win the final. It would be a wonderful end to a great year in his sporting career. Not only that, but he wanted this Welby line-up to be remembered for a long time for doing something special and he knew that his team-mates felt the same way. They all put in the extra effort in the days that led to the final, eager to take whatever Reeves asked of them if it would mean the success they so desired.

It was after Wednesday's training when Guy's team-mates showed him just how much they wanted to win the Cup. He could sense something in the air as the men filed back into the changing room. There was a slight tension, an atmosphere of heightened excitement similar to that he always felt just before a match. As far as he knew, they had all finished for the day and there was nothing important that lay ahead for them. Things became even more suspicious when Guy realised that none of the other players was actually getting changed and instead sat or stood around talking to each other, or remained silent as if waiting for something to happen.

"So, when's it start, Mason?" Stu Edwards shouted out at last.

Guy felt rather bemused. He walked over to Mason and tapped him on the shoulder. "When's what start, Grip?" he asked. "Is there something I don't know about."

Mason wore an open, happy smile. "Word's got round, Guy. About how we improved our gameplay. They all want in on it now. Don't want to lose on Saturday, do we?"

Guy felt suddenly incredibly aroused. All these men were ready to go for it just there and then? It seemed like a dream come true.

"There's only one thing for it, then," he said, slipping his hands into the waistband of his shorts. "I'll have to get my cock out."

Guy lowered his shorts and began to masturbate. A loud cheer went up and he thrilled at being watched by so many people as he played with himself. He quickly got an erection and displayed it proudly to his friends before sitting back down on the bench. He pushed his shorts down to his ankles so he could spread his thighs a little wider, enjoying how his legs pressed against the men on either side of him, and how they eyed him in amusement and delight. Guy watched, amazed, as the men around him followed his lead, rummaging around down the front of their shorts, or lowering them to expose themselves fully. Even Georgie Grant was involved, giving Guy an amiable wink as he tugged away at his gradually filling prick.

Guy looked at the pricks of the men who were to the left and right of him. On one side sat Stu Edwards, a man in his late twenties, with a chunky face and short brown hair. Edwards' body was in good shape, with rounded, filled-out shoulders and sizeable thighs, in between which at that moment stood a proud, thick, veiny cock. Edwards smiled at Guy, as Guy eyed him, giving the very end of his tumescence a few squeezes at the same time. On Guy's other side, Bradley Duckham, a man who matched Gripper Mason in hugeness of body shape, tinkered without embarrassment at a medium-sized dick with a big bulbous head. All the men were checking each other out, looking at what everyone else had to offer and comparing size and shape. The situation felt unbelievably exciting. There were so many erections and so many horny-looking men around. Before long, Guy couldn't stop himself: he reached over to Duckham and took his shaft in hand. Duckham relaxed into the caress, his head rolling back with the onset of mutual pleasure. Almost immediately, Stu Edwards copied the move, gripping Guy's dick and beginning to wank it for him. The three men shuffled together for better access to each other, Guy taking a dick in each hand, and his buddies taking it in turns to wank him and play with his balls. The action felt great, all the more so because it was in the presence of so many others. Guy felt torn between paying attention to what was happening to him and eyeing the wank-fest that was going on all around the room – men in twos, threes or fours circle-jerking, or simply on their own, watching all, beating themselves off without any sense of shame or awkwardness. Guy was unsure just how far his team-mates would go, certain that for many of them it would be the first time they had experienced anything like what they were doing right then. The pleasure he was getting from what was going on there and then was enough for him. Kyle, however, had other ideas, whipping off his shorts completely and walking over to Guy in nothing but his rugby shirt and thick socks.

"Time to give the instigator of all this his just deserts," he said, dropping to his knees. He got a roar of approval as he leaned over Guy and took his friend's cock in his mouth, some of the men standing up and circling the new group to get a better look at the action.

"Fucking brilliant," Duckham grinned, jerking away at his cock as Kyle's head bobbed up and down at Guy's crotch. "Me next!"

Without warning, he suddenly lunged at Guy, planting a firm, ferocious kiss on his lips. Guy was delighted. There was one man on his mouth, one on his dick, and he held a third in his hand. All the while, he was being watched by several other masturbating men, sweaty from their exercise and still in their sports kit.

Suddenly, the door of the changing room swung open. The men stopped what they were doing at once.

"Sorry, guys. Got caught up in a meeting." It was Ron Lambert. He barely flinched at what was going on and Guy guessed that he must've been invited to the gathering. "Looks like I'm not too late, though."

He joined the throng around Guy.

"Come on then, Ron," Guy encouraged him. "Let's have a look."

"All right then, boys," Ron unzipped the fly of his trousers, slipped his hand inside, then pulled out his member and balls. "Don't say I don't do anything for you."

As Kyle returned to his munching, Guy marvelled at how attractive Ron looked. He had always thought Ron a handsome man, secretly holding a desire to see what his body would be like close up and in a state of excitement. Now he had the chance and it didn't disappoint. Ron's manhood was wonderfully rude as it rose to the occasion, looking somehow incongruous pointing out of the front of his trousers. Guy reached over to it to feel it thicken in his hands, causing Ron to nod with approval at the first touch. Soon, all the men were groping each other again in some manner or another, having their hands in each other's groins or touching up their chests, bellies and backsides. Some of them began to kiss, just as Guy and Duckham had, and others squatted in front of each other, taking it in turns to suck each other off. Mason moved behind Kyle, spitting on his fingers before slipping them up his arse. Kyle raised his head, obviously finding the initial insertion slightly uncomfortable, but almost immediately his face melted into an expression of bliss as his pleasure increased.

"That's my boy." Mason gave Kyle a good spank on the buttocks with his free hand, then wiped his hefty cock over the exposed skin in front of him.

Guy was in utter ecstasy at that moment, moving his attentions from team-mate to team-mate, kissing Duckham or Edwards and sometimes both of them at the same time, their heads meeting together at their outstretched tongues.

"All right, I've had enough of your fingers, Mason. I want something else up there," Kyle said, raising his head once more. "Who wants to stick their cock up me?"

The players cheered again, happy at the way things were turning out.

"Well, Guy," Mason stood up, his dick bouncing up and down as he did so. "As Man of this particular Match, I think you should be the one to do the honours."

"Yeah," agreed Georgie Grant. "I want to see that!"

Guy felt no inclination to disagree. He pulled off his shirt, enjoying his nakedness in front of everyone, took a condom and some lube from his bag, then moved around to kneel behind Kyle.

"Go on, Guy," Duckham encouraged. "Give him one for me."

"I'll shut you up," Kyle warned him humorously, before leaning over and taking Duckham's prick between his lips.

Guy rubbered up, carefully applying the lube to himself and to Kyle's arse. He was so horny he didn't feel like taking much time over what he was doing and guessed from the state he was in that neither did Kyle.

Guy slipped himself up his friend, loving the sensation of another man's body opening up and around him. He let Kyle get used to the new probe inside him and then began to fuck, finding that Kyle was already so aroused he could move up to speed almost immediately. He had always enjoyed shagging Kyle and that time was no exception. His pleasure was greatly increased, though, by being surrounded by other men performing sexual acts on each other. There were many cocks in fists or in mouths and he thrilled at being part of what had helped them become erect.

"That looks fantastic!" Lambert, looking downwards, panted at Guy. "Any chance you can give me a bit?"

Lambert let go his dick and moved closer to where the two young players fucked. Guy concentrated on keeping a steady rhythm with his hips, while opening his mouth so that his boss could slip inside him. The prick was good, hard and sticky. Lambert began to slide his shaft in and out of Guy, just as Guy was doing to Kyle, his moans rising to join those of the other men around. Guy felt completely engulfed in sexual activity. There were horny men and erect cocks all around him and it felt great. He would have loved to take the action forever if he could, but before long, his body began to ache for release.

When Stu Edwards, who was being furiously wanked off by Mason, began to come, Guy knew he couldn't last much longer. Stu's spunk flew out of him with great force. It splashed over Guy's torso and Kyle's back, Guy loving the heat of the fluid upon him. Lambert was fucking Guy in the mouth quite readily now and Guy adored taking the man like that. He felt Lambert thicken within him, before he, too, started to shoot and round after round of salty load poured out onto his tongue and the inside of his cheeks.

Then it was his turn. He gave Kyle a few strong bucks to bring himself off and then his dick did all the work. It steeled and his pleasure became almost overwhelmingly intense. All over his body, his muscles tensed before relaxing as he ejaculated. Again and again it pulsated within Kyle's rectum, completely beyond his control, sending out shockwaves of utter bliss throughout his being. The orgasm was fantastic and it all but drained Guy. As he pulled himself out of Kyle's body, he flopped over onto his friend's back just to feel the support of a man's body at such a delicate moment.

It was not the last orgasm to happen during that session and neither was it Guy's last that day. He rested a while, cleaning himself up and replenishing his dehydrated body with water before returning to the action, which was just too good to leave at one shag alone. What made it all the better was that, by now, Guy fully recognised the consequences of what the men were doing. With a sex session so fulfilling, they were surely bound to win the game on Saturday.

Fifteen

The day of the final arrived. Guy felt positive, if not completely without trepidation as he entered the changing rooms. He was eager to get out onto the pitch and his emotions were heightened by the importance of the match and the excitement of the men around him. The team they faced, Darley, were a skilled group of men, who they all knew would be no pushover and who would take all they were capable of to defeat. Lambert's pre-match pep-talk was as encouraging as always, however. He told them, as they all knew deep inside, that they could beat Darley if they played as they had so far that year. Lambert even made reference to the training session the Wednesday previous, making a humourous comment about "teamwork" that got a good laugh from the players. It relaxed them and they went to face their opponents in a bolstered mood, with just enough of an edge of nerves to get the adrenaline pumping around their bodies, priming them mentally and physically for what was ahead.

The cheers of the crowd were like nothing Guy had heard before. They seemed louder than ever, the fans of both sides competing to be heard. The sound boosted his determination even more and, as the opening whistle blew, he just knew he had to do the best he could to prove, once and for all, that he meant business at Welby.

Welby scored the first points early on in the game, but Darley soon won them back. Guy realised then that the match would be pretty even, a struggle rather than a walkover. Darley were on their opponents at every opportunity, but where there was a space to be found, a pass or a tackle to be made, Welby made it. They had the togetherness that Lambert had spoken of, each man working as if he knew what the others were doing, as if they were parts of the same body, every motion in synch with each other. Guy was pleased with what had caused the final improvements in Welby's game, but he didn't have time to think about it much. He concentrated instead on finding his place within the harmonious machine Welby had become and doing his best. Darley played well, but up against what Welby achieved that afternoon, they had little hope. As the final whistle blew, with Welby well ahead, Guy's emotions soared. They had done it! All the work he and his team-mates had put in had finally paid off! They had won the Cup! It felt like the golden culmination of every minute he had had since he had arrived in Welby. As he held up the trophy for the stadium to see and the Welby fans began to chant his name, the moment was confirmed. All the trials and tribulations were worth it and he could be proud of what he and his team-mates had achieved.

A few afternoons later, Guy was walking through Welby's town centre when he received a pleasant surprise. He spotted a familiar face heading towards him through the shoppers. It was Shaw, who saw him and burst into a happy, elated grin.

"Have you heard the news?" Shaw yelled out to Guy as the two of them approached each other.

"What news?" Guy asked, feeling rather bemused.

"The strike. It's over. The deal's off. Production is staying in Welby!"

"You're joking!" Guy exclaimed. "That's wonderful!" Forgetting himself, he grabbed hold of Shaw in sheer delight, taking him into a firm, congratulatory embrace. Instantly, he wondered if he had done the right thing. It was his first moment of physical contact with the man. Shaw had never been particularly tactile before and

Guy suddenly became concerned that he would make the man uncomfortable, especially in surroundings so public. To his relief, however, the embrace was fully reciprocated, Shaw's big strong arms wrapping around him without reticence and in a manner that expressed not a little affection. Time seemed to stop for Guy in those arms. The hug seemed to last beyond the few seconds that celebratory contact would and entered into the realms of a physical encounter that meant much more. Guy felt not simply aroused by being so close to a man he was so attracted to, but deeply moved and warmed by the experience. It felt as if he had found a home in the cradle of Shaw's body.

All too soon, it was over and the two men parted again. They looked at each other, neither of them showing any signs of awkwardness or reserve. All the same, Guy's head felt as if it was somewhere several miles above him and he had difficulty re-starting the conversation.

"Found out this morning," Shaw said at last. There was a new calm in his voice that Guy had not heard before, distinct from either the authoritarian, in-control tones he used outside the factory, or the excited manner he had shown only moments earlier. "We go back to work next week."

"That's fantastic." Guy no longer perceived anyone else around him. All that existed at that moment was Shaw and himself.

"We... I want to do something to thank you for what you've done for us. I thought I could start by taking you on a tour round the factory. You've seen enough of it from the outside."

"I'd love to," Guy murmured. Right then, he would have agreed to just about anything Shaw asked of him.

"We'll have to give things a few days to settle down first, of course. But I'll give you a call and let you know."

"No problem." In that very minute, there were no problems for Guy, absolutely none at all.

Shaw told Guy that he had some things to do around town, so

couldn't stick around long. The two men made their goodbyes and with one final squeeze of Guy's arm Shaw strode off down the main street. Guy watched dreamily until his broad shoulders and easy swagger were no longer in sight.

It sank in over the next few hours that maybe his mother had had some influence in the progress of the deal after all. Guy rang her that evening to get her side of the story, asking exactly what she had said or done to cause such an abrupt change. She was delighted with the news, revealing that all she had done was to invite Hugo's parents round for dinner and explain to them what the effects of the closure would be on Welby. She hadn't lectured them, she said, just put forward a simple and straightforward case. She knew it wasn't as if David needed any more money, being so rich there was nothing else he could do with it, and she guessed that he must've just had a generous change of heart. Guy congratulated her and thanked her profusely for her actions, inviting her up to Welby so she could meet a few of the strike team and become fully aware of the positive effects her actions had had.

The following week, he arrived at the factory for his visit. It felt quite strange to be allowed to drive in through the gates for the first time rather than park up the street from them. As he got out of his car, he became excited, not only because he would be seeing his friends from the strike employed once more, but also because he would be given a chance to see Shaw again.

Guy reported to the factory's reception as had been arranged. The receptionist took Guy's name, signed him in and then rang for Guy's tour guide on an internal phone. Before long, Shaw arrived, and smiling, took Guy's hand a firm handshake.

"Glad you could make it," he beamed.

"So am I," Guy said. It was the first time he had seen Shaw in his foreman's overalls and he was struck by how much the clothing accentuated his masculinity. He was sorely distracted by tempting thoughts of unbuttoning what his friend was wearing so that he could slip his hands inside, but unfortunately there were other matters to be dealt with first.

"Right, if you're ready, we'll get you changed. Don't want you getting your clothes dirty." Shaw directed Guy to a door on the left of the reception desk. Guy followed him through it and down a short corridor to the men's locker room.

Inside, Shaw opened his locker. "I've got a spare pair of overalls for you in here," he said, taking them out and handing them to Guy. "You can just slip them over what you're wearing, or take some of it off. It can get quite warm in some of the rooms."

Weighing up his options, Guy slipped off his jeans, enjoying the brief moment of exposure in front of Shaw. He put on the overalls and the two men moved on.

The first port of call was a large room filled with conveyor belts, at the side of which stood lines of men and women checking the bits of metal that slowly moved past them.

"This is Quality Control," Shaw shouted over the whirr of the machines as he and Guy walked around the edge of the room. "You might recognise some of the faces."

Guy looked around. He did spot a few people he knew and, as they saw him, they waved and shouted his name. Some of them clapped and cheered at him, laughing and making jokes at seeing him in the uniform of the factory. He stopped to speak to them a while, happy to see them obviously feeling secure in their jobs once more and receiving their thanks for his support.

"This next place is a bit more hectic." Shaw led Guy into an adjoining building. "It's where we take care of the bigger stuff."

On entering the room, Guy could feel the increased heat generated by the larger, more complex machinery in it, and he began to sweat. The noise was much louder than the previous room as well, and he and Shaw had to shout over it to make themselves heard. The action was more intense, although Guy could see the care the workers took as they carried out their tasks, directing sizeable metal constructs together, working on them with power tools or welding them together. The work seemed a lot dirtier and demanding than in the previous room, primarily because of the increase in size and weight of what the men were dealing with, and many of them had muck and grease on their hands, clothes and faces and their foreheads dampened with sweat.

"Come to get your hands dirty, eh?" shouted a voice. Guy turned to find his hefty new buddy, Nutter Harris, working nearby. Harris waved a large electrical implement at him. "Fancy a go?"

Guy looked at Shaw for the go-ahead.

"Why not?" Shaw shrugged. "Nobody's looking. Just don't hurt yourself 'cos you won't be insured."

"Nothing major," said Harris as he passed over the mighty tool. "It's just a cog tightener."

Harris directed Guy to a large piece of metal. He showed Guy which button to press and where to place the tightener. Carefully, Guy followed the instructions, surprised at the strength and speed of the thing he held in his hands. He worked on a couple of cogs, Harris making jokes about him being a quick learner and telling Shaw that maybe he could find him a job there. Guy marvelled at how the relationship between him and Harris had changed so much, feeling glad that it had. He noticed how much happier Harris seemed now and guessed that the split that had occurred between him and Georgie Grant had worked out for the best.

Harris winked at Guy as Shaw told the two of them that it was time to move on and, when Shaw wasn't looking, mouthed a silent "Go on!", directing a nod at the foreman to indicate exactly what he meant by the gesture. It seemed that Guy wasn't the only one who would be happy to see him and Shaw together.

"So there you have it," Shaw said as he and Guy left the final part of their tour. "Not the best work in the world, but at least it's work. And a lot of the people here are glad to have it."

"Well, thanks for showing me around. I enjoyed it a lot. It was good to see what everyone I met on the strike team gets up to here." Guy had decided during the tour to ask Shaw out for a drink and the butterflies in his stomach danced with excitement.

"I'm sure they were glad to see you, as well. You've done a lot for them these past weeks."

The two men returned to the corridor near the reception. "I think we need one last stop before I let you leave," Shaw told Guy with a smile. "You're looking a bit dirty, if you don't mind me saying," he explained. "The showers are next to the locker room, if you'd like to take advantage of them."

Guy said he would. He did feel rather grimy, having become quite warm during parts of the tour in the constriction of his overalls.

"I'll join you," Shaw continued as they re-entered the locker room. "I've got the rest of the day off and I'll go home after I've seen you to your car."

Guy began undressing tentatively, all the while feeling the undercurrents of arousal at seeing Shaw's gradually revealed body. He had olive-coloured skin, as if there was some Mediterranean blood in his heritage. He was lean and well-shaped, his limbs and torso looking taut, but not scrawny, and his chest and belly were covered with curls of brown hair. Guy couldn't stop himself from glancing at Shaw's flaccid dick, which danced at its owner's movements, dangling provocatively out of a good bush of pubes. He so desperately wanted to touch it, to possess it as if it was his own, but, not wanting to screw up a delicate moment in their burgeoning relationship, kept his passionate thoughts to himself.

"You can borrow my shower gel," Shaw said as he strode into the showers. "I didn't expect you to bring your own."

Guy began rinsing himself off under the water, wiping some of the grime off his hands and face. He reached over to the water pipe where Shaw had hung the bottle of gel, just as Shaw also reached for it. Briefly, and accidently, the two men's hands brushed against each other.

"Sorry," said Shaw, looking a little uncomfortable. "You first."

Guy squeezed out some gel and started to rub it over his body.

"I was thinking, Guy," Shaw cleared his throat. He looked nervous, displaying a lack of confidence that Guy had never seen in him before. "We should stay in touch. Now that the strike's over."

"I was thinking the same thing," Guy smiled at him, trying to allay his worries.

Shaw paused a few seconds, obviously plucking up the courage to continue. "Maybe... maybe we could go out for a drink sometime. You know, just you and me."

Guy felt as if an explosion of happiness had just been let off inside him. He had been pre-empted.

"I'd love to, Shaw. I think that would be really great."

The two men looked directly at each other for the first time since they had entered the showers. Guy suddenly felt overwhelmed by desire for him. It wasn't just lust he was experiencing, though. That was part of it, for sure. It was borne upon an inescapable need for the two of them to make contact at last on a deep level that could only be expressed physically. There was no avoiding it. Guy had to act.

"But we don't have to wait until then," he said at last.

"For what?" asked Shaw, looking puzzled.

"I think you know," Guy answered. He moved closer to Shaw, placed his hands upon his waist and then kissed him fully on the lips. Thankfully, the move was reciprocated. Shaw responded with a tender mouth and tongue. Almost immediately, Guy felt himself become erect, at the same time feeling Shaw's hardness beating against his lower belly. It was obviously a moment that both men had been waiting a long time for. They pressed closer together and Guy shivered at the meeting of his wet skin upon his lover's. He ran his hands over Shaw's broad back and down to his tight buttocks to drag him further inwards and the two men began to rub their midriffs against each other to pleasure each other at the crotch. Shaw moved to kiss Guy on the neck, then raising his mouth upwards, he whispered in his ear.

"I'm glad you did that, Guy, I would never have dared if you hadn't made the first move."

He leant backwards, looking Guy in the face. "But now I'll dare do anything for you."

"Like what?" Guy grasped Shaw's tight biceps, giving them a squeeze, enjoying their manly hardness.

"Like this." Shaw kissed Guy on the chest. "And this," he repeated the move, only this time lower. "And this," he kissed Guy again, once more lower down his body. "And this," he was now kneeling, his face mere inches away from Guy's fully erect prick. He took hold of it, then softly kissed the tip with as much care as he had used elsewhere on Guy's body. He opened his mouth and took it inside him. Guy thrilled at the warm, wet caress.

Shaw moved further inwards, giving Guy a good, hard suck at the same time. Guy closed his eyes with joy, loving the sensation of what he knew already would be a really good blowjob. He felt Shaw take hold of his balls, tickle them a little, then cup them fully in his hands as he moved his head up and down Guy's shaft. Guy opened his eyes to have a good look at what he was doing and his heart skipped a beat at seeing such an attractive man eating away at his piece. Shaw let the thing escape from him and, excited as it was, it bounced upwards to throb freely a couple of times. He lifted Guy's testicles and began to lick them, before putting them into his mouth and giving them a toothless chew. The feeling was exquisite. Guy stroked Shaw's wet hair and neck. All too soon, Shaw was rising again, but the kiss that replaced the action at Guy's crotch more than made up for its absence. Guy felt utterly wonderful in Shaw's arms. It was as warm and comfortable an experience as it had been in the street those days before, and yet now it was even better as Guy knew his feelings were reciprocated, that their spirits and souls were meeting together as they made love for the first time.

Almost as if they knew what was on each other's minds, both men's hands slipped down to each other's crotches, fondling between their legs, then grabbing hold of each other's hard dicks. They began to wank each other, tenderly at first, then as their pleasure increased, speeding up accordingly. Guy loved the feel of Shaw's hard muscle against his hand, squeezing and jerking away at it and rubbing his fingers over the end to trace the sticky goo that had begun to ooze out of it. He looked down to take his first full look at the thing since it had become erect. It was a big piece and thick, but looked suitably proportioned against Shaw's large frame. It looked delightfully rude, fighting against Guy's fingers, the foreskin that only partially covered Shaw's glans dragging back and forth to reveal a darkly-pink head, shiny with pre-come. Guy took hold of Shaw's hairy, hefty balls as he masturbated him, causing his lover to wince with delight.

With sudden fervour, Shaw pulled Guy towards him into a tight embrace. Their kisses became frantic, as their cocks, pressing against each other, rubbed together. Guy loved the heat and hardness upon him. He was becoming lost in passion now and could only groan when he felt Shaw's probing fingers working their way up the split of his buttocks to his ringpiece. He shivered at the initial tracing of his entrance, then heard himself moan without volition at being opened up. Guy concentrated on relaxing himself to allow Shaw access. It settled, before pulling back and re-entering him once more. Guy felt completely at Shaw's mercy as his finger began to fuck him. He would submit to anything Shaw wanted to do to him just as long as the pleasure went on. Again and again he was penetrated. He sensed himself gradually becoming looser when another finger slipped in alongside the first, stretching him even more and bringing him to even further heights of pleasure. Soon enough, he wanted the two of them to be joined as completely and as meaningfully as they could.

"Fuck me," he murmured in Shaw's ear when he managed to wrest himself from his lover's lips. "Like only you can."

Shaw looked deep into Guy's eyes. Without speaking, he nodded, then ran off back into the locker room. Within seconds he returned, rubbering up quickly. Guy bent over in front of Shaw, resting his hands on his knees for support. He felt a wetness upon his anus as lube was squeezed onto him, then Shaw's fingers spreading it over him, sliding up him much more easily. And then, there it was, the first contact between Guy's hole and the dick he wanted so much to be inside him. Steadily it pushed against him and he worked to accept it, Shaw grabbing him at the waist and dragging him backwards onto his length. It was a beautiful moment. It felt as if Shaw wasn't only filling his rectum, but filling the gap in his soul that up until the point of their meeting, he had barely knew existed. Guy felt the top of Shaw's thighs touch his buttocks, and he realised that Shaw was fully inside him. He would have kept Shaw in that position forever if he could, the two of them joined together, surely as they were meant to be, but still couldn't deny the pleasure caused by Shaw pulling back and beginning to fuck. The man's moves were careful at first, working against the constrictions of Guy's muscles, but they gradually became quicker and soon enough the regular slap, slap of the two men's bodies meeting together echoed around the tiled walls of the shower room. Guy felt ecstatic at having sex with Shaw at last. He knew with every cell of his body that they weren't merely screwing, but making a true and pure connection, that every time their bodies slammed together their pleasure was mutual, felt equally and almost telepathically on both sides and perfect because of that.

Guy felt Shaw lean over him, kissing him on the neck. He turned his head sideways so their mouths could meet. The position was awkward, but it still felt good. Shaw grabbed hold of Guy's dick at the same time. Guy shuddered with utter joy, realising how aroused he had become. It would not be long before he reached orgasm.

"Go on then, man," Shaw encouraged him, still bucking away. "I'm ready, too."

Shaw increased the pace of his shafts, ramming away at Guy hard and fast as he wanked him off. It was as much as Guy could take and almost immediately he felt the final thickening of his cock. He heard Shaw cry out, indicating that he was coming too, as his body was possessed by a spreading current of bliss. He lost himself utterly in his rapture, as his dick began to shoot, pulsation after pulsation racking his body as he felt the spunk fly from him, hitting his lower belly and being rubbed over him by Shaw's fingers. His rectum spasmed again and again, gripping Shaw's jerking cock tighter and tighter as he felt Shaw's final fucks lessen in ferocity as his own orgasm worked its magic. Guy knew right then something special had happened, that it had been caused not just by the sex but by the particular love of one special man.

Guy stood up, feeling rather sorry that Shaw had to pull out, but consoled at being in the big man's arms once again and at having the chance to kiss him fully once more. Something special *had* happened between the two of them, and he knew exactly what it was. He had fallen in love.

Sixteen

Guy shut and locked the door to his flat for what he knew would be the last time. Although he had good memories of the time he had spent there, he was not sorry to move on. It was time for a big change in his life, as big a shift as had occurred when he had moved into Welby and he had a new and bright future ahead of him.

He went downstairs and outside, checking with the men placing his belongings into the removal van that everything was alright. Satisfied, he crossed the road to his own car and got in, feeling more than ready for the move.

"You okay?" Shaw was already in the passenger seat.

"Yeah," Guy answered. "Just feeling thoughtful, I guess."

Shaw tenderly put an arm around him. "Leaving places can make you like that."

Guy smiled at his friend. "I know," he said, then shrugged. "It's not as if I'm going far, though, is it?"

Shaw laughed. "Not really," he agreed. "A new home out in the countryside."

"It's not just *a* home, though," Guy interjected. "It's *our* home and I can't wait to move into it."

The two men looked at each other, then kissed fully and passionately. Guy felt completely settled in Shaw's embrace, finally happy with his life in Welby, feeling at last that he had found somewhere he wanted to stay for a long, long time.

The Masters File
by Jack Dickson

An obsessional journey towards sadomasochism

Living with long-suffering boyfriend Gerry, life is easy for oversexed freelance journalist Gavin Shaw: great job, all his home comforts and the opportunity to indulge in casual sex whenever he gets the itch.

That's when an old flame by the name of James Delany makes him an offer he can't refuse.

While James has varied kinky interests, Gavin shies away from anything which smacks of power-play, and that's why he dropped James like a shot when their brief fling strayed too close to the edge. Still, Gavin is a man who never turns down a dare... A pacy, sexy thriller that travels to the outer sexual limits.

Praise for *Out of this World* by the same author:

'The king of the erotic story' (four stars) *Out in Greater Manchester*

'WOW!!!! ... I was left breathless. A truly great storyteller and a brilliant headf**k' *Scotsgay*

ZIPPER BOOKS/ UK £8.99 US $13.95 (when ordering quote MAS758)